DEATH BY TRIANGULATION

JOHN OUGHTON

NeoPoiesisPress.com

NeoPoiesis Press, LLC

2775 Harbor Ave SW, Suite D, Seattle, WA 98126-2138
Inquiries: Info@NeoPoiesisPress.com
NeoPoiesisPress.com

Death by Triangulation by John Oughton
ISBN 978-0-9903565-0-9 (paperback : alk. paper)

    1. Mystery: Fiction. I. Oughton, John.

Library of Congress Control Number: 2015942946

First Edition

Cover Design: Milo Duffin and Stephen Roxborough

Printed in the United States of America.

Contents

For my daughter Erin

"I think I know enough of hate…"
from "Fire and Ice" by Robert Frost

On January 20, 1961, Robert Frost read a poem titled "Dedication" at the inauguration of John Fitzgerald Kennedy as 35th President of the USA. Kennedy uttered these words: "And so, my fellow Americans: ask not what your country can do for you– ask what you can do for your country. My fellow citizens of the world: ask not what America will do for you, but what together we can do for the freedom of man."

Preface

    This novel was written in fits and starts over several years. I owe debts of gratitude to Centennial College for continuing to employ me during this period; to the Gibraltar Point Artists Retreat and the Tubagua Plantation Eco Village (Dominican Republic) for providing me comfortable accommodations fruitful for writing; and to my family for putting up with my distraction as I tried to puzzle through the difficult business of writing something coherent that is longer than a poem. I also appreciate the many friends who made helpful suggestions (or demanded a cameo), and the advice of Gail Bowen, as Writer in Residence for the Toronto Reference Library, about ways to improve my first 20 pages.

    As is common in fiction inspired by history, there is some overlap between my fictional world and the genuine one. The John Fitzgerald Kennedy assassination and the events following it are seared into the memory of any North American born before it. Any mistakes about this and other historically verifiable events are mine. Further, I am sure that the CIA would never (What, never? Well, hardly ever…) engage in the sort of unethical operations described in this work of fiction. I should add, too, that no member of the Ontario Provincial Police has ever made improper advances to anyone I know.

    E. Howard Hunt's deathbed "confession" really did take place, as detailed in a *Rolling Stone* article (April 5, 2007), and Corsican gangster Lucien Sarti was named in it.

    My book does not purport to be the definitive solution to who really killed President Kennedy and why. It is only one possible explanation, taking into account the latest developments at the time I was writing the novel. We may never know the complete answer. The paradox of the assassination is not that evidence was lacking, but that there was too much, often contradictory, leading investigators to follow many false trails and sometimes come up with analyses as convoluted as the Warren Commission's "magic bullet." It supposedly struck both Kennedy and Governor Connally, changing direction several times.

I didn't write this because I am an abashed admirer of Kennedy's thousand-day presidency. When you look past his glamour and charisma, he seems, like most politicians, a mixture of strengths and weaknesses. He was probably both too young and too flawed to be a great world leader. Yet he had some very contemporary notions about civil rights and the value of democracy, and unlike many born to wealth and power had compassion for the oppressed. This novel is not about him, but about the forces that may have killed him and still operate in today's world.

It's also, I hope, about the quest of a protagonist not totally unlike me to figure out who he wants to be and how he wants to conduct his life. That's another complex mystery.

John Oughton, Toronto, February, 2015

Chapter One

"Great-uncle Gavin is the best-known author shot dead driving a lawn tractor along a highway," Richard Owen told me. If anything could snag my interest in a case, that sentence would. Granted, I'm not all that hard to interest when my bank overdraft is starting to flash red, which is most of the time. I'm a poet and a private investigator; poverty is my business.

"I don't solve murders; that's police work," I told the exquisitely-suited young executive. He passed me his business card, a dignified, gold-engraved showpiece that confirmed his status within his family's business, Owen Investments.

"I'm not hiring you to solve a murder. It was probably an accident." he responded.

"So what brings you to me?"

"A personal recommendation, actually," he replied, touching his discreet silk tie. "I know the Enrights, who said you can keep private business private – and you were quite helpful with their Kerouac theft."

"Yes, that was an intriguing case," I said. It was also lucrative; the Enrights came to Canada as a dirt-poor clan from Yorkshire but through luck and smarts had built a retail, and then a banking, empire. One offspring ran a rare and antique bookstore. An unpublished but very valuable Beat manuscript disappeared from the store's safe.

The Enrights' lawyer, something of a poet himself, had hired me, noting that his clients had the aversion to scandal that accompanies old money. It seemed a lesser family member who worked part-time in the store might be the thief, but the Enrights wanted their problem solved without the assistance of the police or the press.

"I'm pleased they appreciated my help," I replied, idly watching a seagull gliding past my grimy office window. It occurred to me that Jonathan Livingstone was too preppy a name for such an elegant scavenger: Brak or Zert seemed more suitable. "Are you aware that my methods are, well, unique?"

"Yes," he replied. "I've heard that you call yourself a Cultural Systems Investigator, and pattern yourself after that holistic detective created by the author of whatsit, *The Hitch-hiker's Guide to the Galaxy...*"

"Dirk Gently was the detective, and Douglas Adams the author," I clarified. "I also use the Investigative Poetry method invented by Ed Sanders." The name didn't ring a bell with my client, who had probably never heard a Fugs song in his life. Someday they might name a new poetic investigative technique after me, Aaron Miles. Yes, my parents named me long before anyone knew that Air Miles would become a common phrase.

"You look at everything around a case, and sometimes write your report in the form of a poem?" he continued.

"Yes, but I do state the result of my work in plain prose, as well," I replied. "You're obviously a business-oriented person. My approach doesn't concern you?"

"Actually, in this situation, a literary and imaginative mind might be the best thing," he said. "We will pay well for your research, and your public silence."

Pay well! Were sweeter words ever uttered to a poet's ear? As a group, we don't love money alone, or we'd be in bespoke suits ourselves. But we do love the wine, women and other delights it can ease the way for.

"First, though, tell me a little about yourself, besides your investigative methods. One thing I've learned in banking is to know whom I'm dealing with before I sign anything," he stated.

"OK, you want my one-minute Heritage Moment?"

He nodded judiciously.

"Born in small Ontario city with a slow river named the Speed and a half-size replica of the Notre Dame Cathedral on the hill. Youngest of three children. My father sold insurance and my mother designed gardens for people. We went on camping trips across Canada with our grandmother and a series of dumb black and white dogs, all named Tippy. I was a mediocre student because school bored me, until university. Then I got interested and finished a BA in Literature and Cultural Studies. Travelled to Japan and South America. I did some of this and that – drove trucks, worked briefly as a reporter, started to write poetry. I've been a PI for six years now, and to do that, had to prove I have no police record. I'm single and own an old motorcycle and an eccentric art collection."

He smiled and held up his hands in a gesture of sufficiency. I got the impression he was watching my body language more than listening to what I said. I guess I passed his inner lie detector.

"What is it you want me to find out?" I asked.

He leaned back in his chair, sighed, looking tired, and gazed around my (compact, cozy.... small) office. "Don't private eyes always keep a bottle of rye in a drawer somewhere?"

It was going to go on his tab, anyway, so I pulled my bottle of brandy and two balloon glasses out of the "Other Business" drawer of my filing cabinet.

"I can't stand rye. This will have to do," I said.

"Anything," he said gratefully. I poured us each a tot, then watched the colour come into his face.

"How much do you know about my late uncle?" he asked.

"Enough to be aware he makes the rest of you look like very white sheep," I smiled. "Gavin Owen is known for his one great novel, the erotic coming-of-age story *Felt Life Grow*, but some critics think he was one of the most accomplished Canadian poets, too."

"That's very diplomatic," Richard said, loosening his tie. Nothing like brandy to dissolve corporate constraints. "It's thoughtful of you not to mention that he was a notorious anti-Papist, right-wing gadfly, womanizer, and drunk, too. Most of my family left the religious wars behind in Ireland, but not him. He's done enough damage to our name. But now that he's dead, we're afraid his hand might reach out of the grave and smear the family image again."

That was an unfortunate figure of speech, but I refrained

from commenting on it.

"Before I go on, reassure me. Once I've paid you a retainer and we've signed a contract, your secrecy is guaranteed?"

"You've got it," I said, "plus my word." I slid a standard contract across the desk; he wrote "one week" in the time slot, signed it, and extracted from his stylish billfold twenty works of art, freshly printed, each closely resembling a $100 bill. Obviously, he didn't want a paper trail to my services. I could live with that. So could my banker,

"Gavin left broad hints that he had proof of some huge conspiracy, and that the time was coming for the world to learn of it. He claimed this had to do with the murder of a world-famous figure, and he'd kept quiet until nearly all the others involved had died."

"So what was he was going to do – sell it to Fox News?" I asked.

"We don't know what he was going to do with it, or who the supposed victim was," Richard said. "In fact, the whole thing could be a figment of his over-proof imagination, or a plot for the comeback novel he also claimed to be writing. He left hints in some rambling, nonsensical poem in his house in Prince Edward County, but we can't make heads or tails of them." He handed me a folded piece of paper. I opened it and glanced at the first line: "I predict that which is past..." OK, we were playing with paradox here. I decided to put this aside until I could give it full attention.

"What about his death?" I asked, refreshing his brandy glass. "Could that be a clue?"

"Frankly, we don't know," Richard replied. "A lot of people disliked him, but those who hated him would probably have done him in years ago, when he was actively issuing paranoid screeds and letters to the editor. The police say the bullet that killed him was a 30-06, typical of a hunter's rifle, and it was deer season there. Unless the OPP find a motive, they're betting a stray round missed a white-tail and got him... while he was riding his Kubota lawn tractor to town." I wondered about the odds of a stray bullet hitting a target moving at 15 klicks or so, but decided to leave that one to the cops.

"And why was he using that mode of transport?" I asked,

more from idle curiosity than any feeling that this was important.

"Oh, he was nabbed driving drunk so often that they took away his license for life," Richard replied. "He was getting too old for his bicycle, and the lawn tractor was all he had left. He wouldn't take taxis except in dire need. Few cabbies understood that the only worthwhile opinions were his, not theirs."

He shot a cuff to consult the watch that gleamed dully on his wrist. You know the way old gold doesn't shriek its presence, just radiates a self-assured glow?

"I'm afraid I have another appointment, so I'll cut to the chase." He dropped an old skeleton key on my desk, and an envelope. "I'm his executor. This key opens the front door to his house, the only yellow one on a dead-end road. There's a map in the envelope too. I want you to start by going there. Learn what you can. Find out if his neighbours knew anything. There's also a letter asking whom it may concern to help you on behalf of our family. Let me know if it's going to take more than a week. If you find any evidence of this grand conspiracy whatsoever, especially proof that he was involved, I want you to bring it to me."

"Even if it involves a crime?" I said.

"I wouldn't want you to do anything illegal, like suppress evidence" he replied. "But I find it hard to believe that the Ontario Provincial Police, or anyone else, would have more than scandal-mongering interest in something that may or may not have happened forty-some years ago."

I lifted my eyebrow at that. For a vague conspiracy, he seemed to have a precise window of time in mind. My intuition was saying there was something there. I was soon to find out how big a secret the old boy had been playing hide-and-seek with.

But had he been murdered? The sad truth is people disappear, or are killed, all the time. But certain cases, given unique circumstances or the victim's fame, are never satisfactorily resolved. They stick in the public mind. In the States, Judge Crater's vanishing act comes to mind. The demises of Elvis and Marilyn Monroe have been tabloid fodder for decades. In Canada, a good candidate is wealthy theatre impresario Ambrose Small, who disappeared one evening in Toronto in 1919, the day that he had deposited a one-million dollar cheque. Apparently, the butler didn't do it.

Romance surrounds the fate of flier Amelia Earhart and her navigator; only recently did improved DNA testing reveal that the long-sought "survivor" of the Romanov dynasty, Anastasia, had in fact died with her relatives in that gruesome Bolshevik massacre of the Czar's brood. And their little dog, too. Would the death that Gavin Owen *might* have had some part in be as controversial as Anastasia's?

I stared at Richard, wondering what he might be holding back. With humans, there's always something. Damn, I was starting to think like a lawyer.

Richard returned my gaze and stood. "Before you ask, no, I'm not drinking and driving. My uncle did enough of that for several generations. I have a chauffeur."

He shook my hand and left.

I have an old Yamaha motorcycle. But it's more reliable and has more character than any chauffeur I've met. Soon, it'd be taking me to Prince Edward County, home of wineries, huge sand dunes, beaches, farms... and lately the idle rich, from what I'd heard.

I needed to know more about this place before I went. The Beat/Zen/nature poet Gary Snyder once recommended that, to practice their art, poets should learn everything about the world around them: the names of birds, insects, trees, flowers. Anything could be useful, and it's important to know the correct names for what nature offers us, rather than calling a merganser a duck or Queen Anne's Lace a weed.

I'd taken his words to heart. In the city, of course, there were things beside wildlife to learn about. I was an incurable observer and retainer of facts.

I'd learned, for example, about the flat grey metal boxes discreetly placed under the leading edge of Toronto subway stations. They held the necessary supplies for dealing with suicides. I also knew, from a brief stint reporting for a newspaper, that the media had a deal with the Toronto Transit Commission and police not to report ordinary subway suicides, despite their frequency. The rationale was to avoid suggesting this method to potential copycats. I knew that the Roman capital letter "A" was originally upside down and the glyph for the head of the sacred Egyptian bull Apis, whereas capital "B" is thought to have stood for a two-story house (or a window over a door); the Hebrew for house, *beth*, begins with "B".

Another fact cluttering up my consciousness was that Lewis Carroll never wrote a book titled Alice in Wonderland; it's *Alice's Adventures in Wonderland*. How does all this relate to solving cases? You never know until you know. That's what being holistic means to me – don't reject any knowledge out of hand. I'll pass on the macrobiotic sprouts until my next lifetime.

Chapter Two

For me, a case begins with research. I try to keep my mind and senses open when investigating. But unless I have some idea of the context in space and time of what I'm looking at, I could miss clues that later could be crucial.

I took a longer look at Gavin's parting poem. Not the great man's best work, but then it was probably written more to pull a few tails than please critics.

THE RETURN OF (COSA) NOSTRA DAMN-US-ALL

> I predict that which is past
> Not that yet to come
> For the first fixes the last
> And that's an irrational sum
>
> Ergo, sing we now Mr. Flanders Dog
> Who couldn't keep it in his pants
> And the three-way end made of him
> By all parties in the dance
>
> There was the non-Bouchard butcher
> The last word in non-existentialism
> Who packed more power than the patsy
> Into an almighty head-state schism
>
> There was the one who missed
> And the loser of Oz who got kissed

By the ruby lips of rage –
Weren't we the talk of the age?

To follow my path in this
Ask the (w)rapt shrink who held fast
When others abandoned the ship of me
Adrift in seas of rum and sodomy

These are not quite last words
Leave we those to the birds.
Not all hunts find their prey
Read and riddle me another way

Well, Cosa Nostra was a pointer to the Mafia. Could this be alluding to an organized crime hit? Maybe he was playing footsy with the grave of Jimmy Hoffa? As for rum and sodomy, I doubted that, as a staunch proponent of the Orange Order, he was much of a Pogues fan. He probably didn't like Winston Churchill either, who coined the description of the Royal Navy's traditions, with the addition of "the lash". And what's with Flanders? Flanders and Swan? Flanders Fields? Ned Flanders from *The Simpsons*? Somehow I couldn't see the literary scourge of the Papacy taking in many Homer and Marge episodes.

There were obviously other hidden meanings in the poem, but I decided to just let them percolate awhile.

Right now, I needed to know more about two subjects: Prince Edward County – a place I'd never visited – and Gavin Owen and his clan. I fired up my ageing computer, and asked my favourite meta-search engine, Dogpile.com, to "go fetch".

Well, well. Prince Edward County, named for the profligate son (and brief successor) to Queen Victoria, hangs off the shore of Lake Ontario around Belleville, about 200 km east of Toronto. Technically a peninsula, it was joined to the mainland by a narrow tract called Carrying Place because Natives and, later on, voyageurs portaged their canoes there. This is transected by a canal, but two swing bridges allow access to the County, as does one large bridge from Belleville, another near Deseronto, and the ferry at Glenora.

Although native groups, most recently the Mohawks and Mississaugas, lived there for some 12,000 years, most County locals will tell you it was settled in 1784. About 500 Loyalists with assorted mustered-out British and German soldiers arrived on ships. The Loyalists, lacking revolutionary zeal, would rather have seen the USA stay under the protection of the British Crown than be run by wild-eyed democrats.

They found a heavily forested landscape with some excellent agricultural land and a few geologic anomalies, including "the largest baymouth sandbar separating freshwater in the world." This is now Sandbanks Provincial Park, famous for its giant dunes and beaches. The area became a supplier of wheat and barley to the rest of Canada and the US, then market-gardening and food-canning, and finally morphed into a *Vin du Qualité Assuré* wine area, with many small wineries. The climate is tempered by the lake and the soil favours vine-growing. Traditionally a rural and conservative society, it had begun to change with a recent influx of moneyed, older immigrants from Toronto, Ottawa and Kingston. Gourmet restaurants, wine-tasting tours and pretentiousness were the new cash crops.

It has one sprawling, sizeable town, Picton; a couple of thriving villages Bloomfield and Wellington; and two airports associated with the military. Thousands of Allied airmen once trained at the old airfield on Macaulay Mountain, overlooking Picton. Gliders piloted by Air Force cadets and bigger planes full of parachutists still took off from the Mountainview facility along the highway to Belleville.

That was enough research. My head was starting to ache, and there's nothing like a long motorcycle ride in the crisp, lambent air of October to clear it. I packed up my notebooks and camera, threw some spare clothes and a toothbrush into my saddle-bags, and called the few friends who'd miss me, letting them know I'd be out of town for a few days. The last one was Sarah, my favourite red-haired librarian and sometimes girlfriend ... well, she's a woman, but "woman friend" grates on the ear. Maybe I could con her into doing the Owens research.

"You won't believe this," I told her, "but I have a case and money, too. In fact, I've already been paid for a week's work."

"You mean an actual job? Be still, my beating heart," she laughed. "Does this mean you can pay me back the last loan?"

"That and more," I said. "My crystal ball shows champagne, lobster and bouquets for you as soon as I'm back from a road trip to Prince Edward County."

"That's good," she said. "I'll keep myself warm for your return, then."

"Especially my favourite parts, I hope," I said. "Could you do one little favour for me?"

"As long as it's not another loan," she teased.

"Find out what you can about Gavin Owen, the writer, and dump it in an e-mail to me."

"Whaddya think I am, a librarian? Oh, I am. I will," she promised. "But you owe me ... and not just for the loan and Owen," she said.

"I always owe you, just for associating with me. See you in a few days. Love ya."

"Ya back," she whispered, and broke the connection.

There's not much to tell about the ride along the 401 East. I was too busy with the usual biking business – the secret to staying alive on the road – keeping well clear of big trucks that not only leave turbulent wakes but also chuck parts of their tires, or loads, at unwary riders. I had to watch for the many terrible drivers who tailgate at high speed, drift across lanes, text or talk while ignoring the scenery whizzing past at 120 kph, suddenly slow down or speed up for no apparent reason, and never figure out what turn signals are for. I used my old bike's instant power to pull away from these accidents-waiting-to-happen. I would rather stay ahead of trouble than have it bite me in the butt.

Then there are the front-wheel-eating pot holes, badly-filled cracks that force sudden steering changes, stretches of grooved surface, and the random surprises of dropped oil and loose gravel on the pavement. To live past your twenties and still ride bikes means achieving a kind of moving meditation, in which you watch everything around you, consider scenarios for the stupidest things drivers could do – because once in a while, they meet expectations – and check the bike's engine sound and stability.

Even so, a steady blast at 120 had my face in a permanent

smile and my ears ringing by the time I exited at Wooler Road, just before Trenton. I didn't see one sheep, though.

I stopped in at a service station cafe – always a place for fine dining. The locals suddenly went quiet in that eerie way country people do when a stranger appears. The fact that I was wearing an orange leather jacket and carrying a full-face purple helmet probably didn't help either. I scanned the menu, with its variations on the thousand things to make with fried meat, and opted for pie and coffee.

Then, I spread out the map Richard had given me and checked my turns again. OK, over the bridge and into The County. I wonder when it became "The", instead of just "a", County.
Anyway, my route turned left on County Road 18, through Ameliasburg, onto Hwy. 62 below the Mountainvew airport, then cut east again on 14 to a hamlet with the unlikely name of Demorestville. *DEMorestville*? *DeMORestville*? I'd have to ask someone the right pronunciation. The patrons here looked more inclined to rope me onto the hoods of their pick-up trucks, though, so I left.

Once over the bridge to the County, the landscape was subtly different. Gently rolling, it revealed prosperous-looking farms, frame houses set back in the words, and a lake reflecting the cumulus clouds. The road to Ameliasburg was a delight, fast and straight past farms and stables, and then suddenly pitching a series of sharp 90-degree turns that seemed to be there for the hell of it, or to follow some wandering boundaries. I remembered that a better poet than Gavin Owen had lived here a long time, and might be buried here: Al Purdy, poet laureate of beer halls, wandering, and northern landscapes. I found a road down to a cemetery dotted with weeping willows, and there it was, a marble slab commemorating the "Voice of the Land."

I communed with a few of his lines in my head for a moment:

> "The worth of life being not necessarily noise
> we kept unusual silence, and then cried out
> one word which has never yet been said…"

I rumbled on through the sleepy, vaguely depressing hamlet of De-whatever-ville, cut north toward Big Island and its wide marsh, and soon was arcing onto Gematria Road.

Richard was right about it being easy to find; even without the new 9-1-1-friendly numbering system, it was the only bright yellow house.

I pulled up, cut the engine, and pulled off my helmet. As my ears began to return to normal, I could hear a few birds calling, a chainsaw somewhere nearby, and then nothing. You don't often get to hear nothing in the Big Smoke. I savoured it.

Owen's house was a rambling affair, two stories in the middle, with a single-story addition tacked onto one side. A fieldstone chimney poked out of the cedar shake roof.

Yellow police tape across the front door rustled in the breeze. I walked around the place, admiring the collection of rusted bicycles, stacks of firewood, broken-down washing machines, and a dented lawn tractor sitting under a lean-to. A brown smear across its hood suggested blood. I looked at the distant fence that probably marked the back of his property, with a stand of maples behind it.

I heard a car pull up, and when I returned to the front of the house, a blonde and businesslike OPP officer was surveying me through the open driver's window. A German Shepherd, almost as large as the officer, sat alert in the passenger seat.

"Help you?" she asked, in a tone that suggested help could extend to dog bites, cuffs, and a rear-seat ride if she didn't like the answer.

"Umm, maybe," I said, and started to reach inside my jacket for the letter Richard had given me.

They must be training officers in quick-draw technique, because I found myself looking at a semi-automatic handgun next.

"How about you slowly open that jacket, show me what you're so anxious to grab, and then we'll start over?" she suggested.

Shootings really ruin a new relationship. I complied. I drew Richard's letter out with my left thumb and finger, keeping my right hand in the air, and gave it to her.

After she'd read the letter and checked my PI licence from the Ministry of the Solicitor General and Correctional Services, she stepped out of her cruiser.

"I'm Constable Lemieux. Sorry to be a little jumpy there," she apologized, offering me a firm handshake. "After Mr. Owen's death, we had a break-in reported, so you can understand my caution."

I looked down the road, and an elderly lady scrutinizing me with impressive binoculars from the verandah of her tiny pink house gave me a little wave. No wonder I'd been busted as soon as I arrived.

"No problem," I answered. "Plus you probably don't get many private investigators here."

"Nope," she said. "Private inebriators are more of a problem."

I smiled at that. Police officers with a sense of humour are pretty rare, from my jaundiced two-wheeler's viewpoint.

"I'm not a PI full-time," I said. "I'm also a poet."

She smiled in return and said, "I don't suppose you're carrying your poetic license, too?"

"Nope." There must be a snappy comeback to that, but I'd have to work on it later. "Was anything taken during the break-in?" I asked.

"We don't know," Lemieux answered. "Some of the place had been tossed, but not destroyed. The odd thing is more what wasn't taken. He had a case of good Scotch, a newish TV set, a collectible samurai sword, and a few hundred bucks stuffed behind a couch cushion. All the things you'd expect a burglar to go for were left behind."

I was about to ask who called it in when I realized I'd probably seen the good citizen already. "Let me guess," I said. "It was reported by a nice little old lady with binoculars."

"You got it," Constable Lemieux replied. "I don't think the perp had long here. Mrs. Bailey is pretty vigilant."

"I couldn't help but notice your four-legged friend there," I said. "Are you a – what's the right term – canine-assisted officer?"

"No, Scout's regular partner's away, so I'm just entertaining him. But I like dogs."

I pulled Owen's ditty out of my saddlebag and checked it again. "Ever hear of a Flanders Dog?"

She reached a finger under the sweat brim of her hat and

scratched. "Ummm… I don't know a breed called Flanders. You mean a Bouvier? They were bred in Flanders to herd cows and do other farm work."

Well, that sounded helpful. But decoding the whole poem was going to require more than just a dog breed name.

"I'll leave you to it," Constable Lemieux said, watching my thoughtful expression with interest. "If anyone else tries to break in while you're here, call us."

"How about if I get scared of the dark?" I replied.

"Then call your mommy. Remember, flirting with a provincial officer is a felony," she said sternly, then winked and drove away.

What is it about me and women in authority? First librarians – who can quiet anyone – and now a cop with a gun and large dog. What's next? A heavy date with a dominatrix?

I stepped over the yellow tape, checked the faded welcome sign over the door ("Abandon Pope All Ye Who Enter Here"), unlocked the heavy front door, and stepped into musty darkness.

Chapter Three

Once I found the light switch, I looked around. Inside my head, I heard Bette Davis sneer "What a dump." The bottom floor was open-concept, essentially one big room with a kitchen nook in one corner, a TV and stained brown corduroy couch in another, and a large pine table littered with papers and books. To my surprise, it also supported a venerable desktop computer, inkjet printer and modem. There was a battered boom-box with a CD player. The old coot had been more technologically advanced than I'd expected. Having read some of his prose about religion, politics, and the world's unfairness, I'd have expected his writing tools to be a goose quill and bottle of vitriol. Another interesting thing: there was no phone anywhere that I could see.

I flipped open what looked like quite an old and well-consulted book on the table. Bound in leather and penned by one Alexander Hislop, it had the long-winded title *The Two Babylons or The Papal Worship Proved to Be the Worship of Nimrod and His Wif*e. Sounded like a best seller, especially if your name was Nimrod. A couple of passages caught my eye: "The Pope himself is truly and properly the lineal descendant of Belshazzar." If I were descended from someone named that, I'd keep it quiet, too. The second passage declared that Catholicism "… must be stripped of the name of a Christian Church." Whew!

I turned on the computer and, after some chugging and whirring, it displayed a normal-looking screen. But I when I tried to check his documents and e-mail, I was confronted by a password request. Nothing I could think of worked, including Hislop and Belshazzar, worked, so I gave up for the time being.

As far as décor, the place was overdue from a visit by Scottish designer twins. The main artwork was a large banner across one wall proclaiming "The Loyal Orange Association". Next to it was a badly-painted oil of a long-haired man waving a sword from a prancing white stallion's back. I presumed this was none other than William of Orange. The samurai sword Constable Lemieux had mentioned hung on another wall, beside a large photo of Yuko Mishima haranguing troops, probably just before his ritual suicide. The whole place smelled like mouldy books, with a hint of decaying food.

The kitchen sink was full of fast-food boxes and dirty dishes.

One of the lesser-known skills in the inventory of a holistic detective is cleaning. You don't want to do it too often, because it can distract from the real task at hand. But at certain stages, a mechanical and repetitive task frees the mind to wander between known facts and intuitive possibilities. Also, you find things in unexpected places where long-term dust bunnies and mutated bacteria lurk.

So I sorted out the trash, finding one interesting thing – an empty prescription vial for Halcyon, with the prescribing doctor's name smudged. I rolled up my sleeves, squirted in some no-name detergent, and washed the dishes.

That done, I scanned the bookshelves: an eclectic mix of modern literature (with some good first editions), mostly fiction; classics by Shakespeare, Chaucer, and the other usual suspects; works on politics and religion with a right-wing, anti-Catholic bent, and a peppering of travel and biographical tomes.

One book caught my eye and I riffled its pages. It was an exploration of the Kennedy dynasty, starting with patriarch Joe and his early days in bootlegging, and following political shakers John, Bobby, and Teddy through their various triumphs and tragedies. On the flyleaf, someone else had written HAH! in heavy black ink. The book included a picture of JFK's wedding, with a caption that rang a bell: "The former Jacqueline Bouvier becomes…" Bouvier? As in Jackie Lee Bouvier Kennedy Onassis? Was JFK the "Mr. Flanders Dog" alluded to in Owen's ditty? Or Jackie's father, whoever he was? I doubted it.

But if this case was going to involve me with either the Kennedy or Onassis clans, I'd kill old Gavin all over again. Between those two families were scandals, conspiracy theories and lawsuits enough to fill the Blackberries of a hundred lawyers until eternity. Although I just wanted a quiet little literary puzzle, I had the feeling I wasn't going to get one.

So what now?

One thing I learned in university: when in doubt, a quotation never hurts. Ed Sanders wrote in *Investigative Poetry: The Content Of History Will Be Poetry*, "Investigative poesy is freed from capitalism, churchism, and other totalitarianisms; free from racisms, free from allegiance to napalm-dropping military police states–a poetry adequate to discharge from its verse-grids the undefiled high energy purely-distilled verse-frags, using every bardic skill and meter and method of the last five or six generations, in order to describe every aspect (no more secret governments!) of the historical present, while aiding the future, even placing bard-babble once again into a role as shaper of the future." Oddly, this reminded me of Gavin's line "I predict that which is past."

So I needed to construct the historical present and then "frag" it. Fair enough. I connected my laptop to the modem and I was in. I found an email from Sarah waiting, detailing her research.

Gavin Owen: born Orangeville, Ont., 1940. Third of four children of Philip and Margaret (née Farley) Owen, who emigrated from Belfast, Ireland, to Canada in the 1930's. BA, Poli. Sci., McGill; MA, Eng. Lit., U of T. Little known about years immediately after MA completion; seems to have roamed US and Canada. Taught at private high schools and a few colleges in Ontario; fired for dispensing political/religious views inappropriately. Appointed Poet Laureate of the Loyal Orange Order of Ontario, 1981. Settled in 1993 in rural Prince Edward County. Convicted of DUI several times there; driver's license suspended for good after the last one. Author of five works of poetry, all from different publishers; one novel, *Felt Life Grow* (described by a critic as "the horny male equivalent of *By Grand Central Station I Sat Down and Wept*"), which has been reprinted six times, and a variety of articles and monographs on formal poetry, tradition and the Catholic church.

No known offspring. Rumoured to have had affairs with wives of politicians and other leading writers."

I went to thank her with a call on my cell... and discovered I'd left it in Toronto. Sometimes my mental absences amaze me. But then I forget about them. I emailed my thanks, and another promise to treat her well on my return to Toronto.

Hmmm... there were a lot of "Orange" strands in Owen's life, starting with his place of birth, and extending to the banner on his wall. Wasn't it the Orange Order that used to incite riots against Irish Catholic immigrants to Canada, keeping the Troubles alive here? Didn't they hold the annual parade in Toronto with someone sitting in for William of Orange on a white horse? I checked the Order on the Web. It started in Northern Ireland in 1795, its members termed "the storm troopers of the Tories." Many Orangemen moved to Canada, reaching their greatest influence around World War I.

But by now, the Order seemed a mere vestige of its former, Catholic-bashing self. Its website defensively proclaimed respect for all religions, while affirming good Protestant family values. This reminded me of the site for the Outlaws biker gang, which insisted its members respected the law, although a name like "Law Abiders" wouldn't have the same resonance on their patches.

Judging by the sign over Owen's door, his attitude towards the Catholic Church had not lost much edge. *Why would an apparently intelligent man hold so firmly to an antiquated prejudice?* I wondered.

Curious, I turned on the CD player to hear the last tune that Owen had danced to. It started in the middle of a song that sounded like the Irish classic "Too-Ra-Loo-Ra –Loo-Ral" although the lyrics were rather different.

...But Bob, the deceiver, he took us all in
He married a Papish called Bridget McGinn
Turned Papish himself and forsook the old cause
That gave us our freedom, religion and laws
Now the boys in the place made some comment upon it
And Bob had to fly to the province of Connacht

Well, he fled with his wife and his fixings to boot
And along with the latter his ould Orange Flute

At the chapels on Sundays, to atone for past deeds
He'd say Paters and Aves and he counted his beads
Till, after some time, at the priest's own desire
Bob went with his ould flute to play in the choir
Well, he went with his ould flute to play in the mass
But the instrument shivered and sighed, oh alas,
And blow as he would, though it made a great noise
The flute would play only "The Protestant Boys"…

Enough of that. I popped the CD out, and found the title of the song was, no surprise, "The Ould Orange Flute."

A quick survey of the upstairs bedrooms turned up more books and the fact that Owen was no slave to laundry duties. I decided to go to the ultimate authority to answer some of my questions: *la dame aux binoculars* down the road.

I walked over and knocked on her door. After a pause, a voice screeched: "If you're selling anything, take a hike. I ain't in a buying mood."

"Not selling," I said. "Just asking about Mr. Owen, who used to be your neighbour. I'm the guy you called the cops on."

The door swung open, and I was confronted by a woman brandishing an iron frying pan. She stood no more than five feet, stooped, with frizzy pinkish hair. Her watery blue eyes gleamed with the light of a person in command of her faculties, including a sharp tongue.

"And why should I be answering you?" she countered.

I went through the rigmarole of the letter and my ID, and her expression softened.

"If it's for his family, I'd be glad to help. And I guess if that nice Constable Lemieux didn't plug you, you're housebroken enough to let in. I'm Doretta Bailey, but you call me Mrs. Bailey until I know you better."

She ushered me into her cluttered kitchen, and made us cups of terrible instant coffee with condensed milk on the side, like a latte-drinker's nightmare. A black and white portable TV set flickered soundlessly on a bureau.

"Gavin Owen," she said. "Now there was a piece of work."

"You didn't like him?"

"Don't think he much wanted to be liked. But I'll say this for him – he never pretended to be better than he was. He was a Mick-hating drunk, fornicator and a reprobate. He would have described himself to you the same way."

"Did you read any of his books?"

"Not likely," she snorted. "My eyes ain't up to much reading these days, so I save 'em for large print romances and history novels, not the dirty ravings of some broke down Scotch-soaked poet."

She did have a way with description.

"What can you tell me? Do you know who might have wanted to kill him?"

"I couldn't say. According to him, lotsa people hated him. But other than you and that burglar the other night, I haven't seen many people around his place. I couldn't tell you who his enemies are."

"If you don't know his enemies, how about friends?" I asked.

"Well, when he first moved in, he still had a few woman visitors. I wouldn't call them ladies, though," she said with a nicely arched eyebrow. "Lately, his only friend was Doc Hagerty."

"What kind of doctor is he?" I asked, thinking of the pill vial I'd found.

"This kind," she said, circling an index finger in the air and then tapping her forehead. "What the Brits call a trick-cyclist."

Aha – one more clue in the poem began to make sense: "(w)rapt shrink"– could Dr. Hagerty be Owen's confidante, the one to ask in the poem?

After ascertaining that Hagerty lived about ten minutes away, somewhere between Demorestville (which according to Mrs. Bailey was DUH-more-est-ville) and Picton, I took my leave. I had a lead. That was enough for one day of detecting, so I went back to Owen's house, poured a Scotch from his case of Glenlivet, and toasted Gavin's memory. He was a cranky SOB, at least in his writing, but he did just buy me a drink. I sat in the back yard listening to the birds until the sun went down. Then, I moved my bike around the back, on general principles. I once had a wonderful purple Triumph Daytona 500 stolen right off my sidewalk in downtown Toronto.

Back inside the house, I recalled how different country nights are. There's almost no sound except for wind moaning around the corners of the house, distant dogs barking, trees rubbing against the house, and a very occasional vehicle going by. It's so quiet you can hear your circulation going (the low sound) and the whine of your nerves working (the high one).

It made me restless, so I performed one of my holistic poet tricks. I turned off all the lights, sat down in the middle of the living room rug, and just felt the house. Psychics say that troubled spirits leave traces of energy where they lived. I've never seen ectoplasm, but I do believe that, by focusing, you can tell something about the person who lived in the house. What could be troubling an old man so much that he'd be on anti-depressants? Perhaps Dr. Hagerty would clear that one up, if his code of ethics allowed him.

The other thing that struck me was what a contradictory mix of elements Owen had been: a well-educated and literate bigot; a womanizing loner. His parting poem obviously wanted to tell us something, but why cloak it in such a mélange of double meanings and obscure references? Why not just say Bouvier or Kennedy instead of "Mr. Flanders Dog?"

Suddenly my attention shifted. I had heard a car come slowly down the road and then cut its engine. I heard crunching gravel as it turned into the driveway beside the house – the one that the Bailey binoculars couldn't reach. But there was no sound of its door opening.

The burglar was back? Here was another puzzle. What of Owen's would someone want badly enough to come back for, risking arrest?

I got up quietly and felt beside along the wall until I found the samurai sword hanging there. I hefted it – it was beautifully balanced, the edge very sharp. I don't carry a gun and rarely need a weapon while on investigations. This would have to do. I had a flash of Bruce Willis considering the same weapon in the pawn-shop scene of *Pulp Fiction.*

I waited in silence while someone worked on the side window. After a brief protest of rending wood, the window was levered up. I waited until I saw a dark figure coming in with a tiny light strapped to his head. I wound up and gave him a good smack on the forehead with the flat of the blade.

He swore, but instead of retreating, dove into the room and then tried to stand. I kicked him medium hard in the temple and he went down. My foot hurt. Even though PI's are supposed to indulge in regular fisticuffs, it's not my specialty.

I turned on a lamp to check my catch. He was medium-height, muscular, dressed in black, and wearing a clichéd crook's balaclava. I had broken the head lamp he was wearing, and a thin trickle of blood appeared as I wrested off the balaclava, but he was breathing steadily. His face was Caucasian, early middle-aged, regular; he had a dimple in his chin, no facial hair, heavy black eyebrows. I wrested a handgun from the holster, a big semi-automatic as impressive as Constable Lemieux's. I had no rope or cuffs, so quickly bound his wrists with the only thing I could find – masking tape. I stuffed his gun into my pocket, went outside and checked his ride – a nondescript mid-size sedan.

I could see Mrs. Bailey's lights still on in her house, so I ran there. I knocked on her door.

She opened it a crack, and said "You again?" but when she heard my rushed account of the burglary attempt she led me to her rotary-dial phone and stood there while I phoned 9-1-1. I got promised a cruiser immediately.

I thanked Mrs. Bailey and ran back to the house, but the burglar had recovered. A few clues told me: first, he and the car were gone; second, he'd printed on the pine table in red magic marker: "LEAVE OR DIE FUCKER!" I think he needed a comma there.

Siren going and lights flashing, the cruiser arrived in a few minutes.

Instead of lovely Lemieux, I got a no-nonsense male cop, who looked skeptical during my story until he inspected the broken window and table-top inscription. I handed him the gun butt-first, remembering my manners. He sniffed the barrel and then placed it in an evidence Baggie.

"Too bad you didn't cut his head off... then we'd have more evidence," he said.

I think he was joking.

"Did you get his license plate?" he asked me, notebook poised.

"Umm... no. I was in too much of a hurry to call you. I haven't found a phone here. I can tell you it was a dark midsize sedan," I said lamely.

"Ever watch *Monk*? I guess you're another defective detective," he said. "Never mind. You might think of staying somewhere else tonight. This house is turning into a high-crime area."

I took his advice and, after boarding up the window with plywood, rode down the road to the highway, where I paid a no-tell motel cash for a room with lumpy mattress, a Gideon Bible, a porn cable channel, and no burglars. And so to bed.

Chapter Four

The next morning, I woke up smelling as if I'd been sleeping in an ashtray. My foot still hurt where I'd kicked the intruder, who must have a hard skull indeed. But there was one positive thing about the motel – no one came through the window.

After a breakfast in its café, which recalled the glories of grease, I got back on my faithful steed and returned to the house. Just as I was setting my bike on its center stand, a car pulled over on the wrong side of the road and stopped. I recognized the sign stuck to its roof, a rural mail delivery contractor's.

When I explained who I was, the driver handed me the mail – a mix of bills and magazine subscription come-ons. He was happy to give me directions to Hagerty's home, on a rural route with the amusing name of Frog Lake Road.

And good directions they were, since after bombing some delightful turns past derelict houses, marshes, and farms, I found the lane to Hagerty's easily enough. It wound back through a maple stand, eventually revealing a small, tidy frame house.

As I rolled up, the front door opened, revealing a slight, white-haired man with a pipe in one hand (the smoking kind, not lead) and a kindly face.

"Sorry," he said. "I've sworn off treating bikers."

When I detailed my mission and showed him Richard's letter, he grew more serious. "You'd better come in," he said. "I've been expecting someone like you since I heard of Gavin's passing."

We sat down in a living room furnished with some surprisingly good modern paintings. I wouldn't have expected a Jack

27

Bush original on Frog Lake Road. An industriously ticking, pendulum-swinging oak and brass grandfather clock in one corner tracked the hour and the phases of the moon.

"Was he your patient, if confidentiality allows you to tell me?" I ventured.

"I don't think he ever made a secret of it," he sighed. "I treated him for a year when he was trying to deal with his alcoholism. Eventually, he realized he liked drinking more than what he called 'the dull edge of reality's knife.' He told me my treatment was a success, but the patient was a failure. But we became friends... he used to drive over here on his lawn tractor."

"The family suspects he may have been sitting on some major scandal, and they've hired me to verify that," I said.

"And probably keep it from the circling media vultures, too?" he suggested.

I nodded. "I like to start by understanding a person as much as I can," I said. "Once you know the context, then any clues you discover might make sense."

"Spoken like a true student of the human mind," he said. "Psychiatry's not that different."

"Let's start with one obvious paradox," I said. "Why would an educated man harbour such a deep hatred of Catholicism?"

"That mystery I can solve," he said. "When Gavin was a lad, he was inseparable from his friend Jimmy. Gavin often told me later that Jimmy was the one person who could read his mind."

"Do you think they ever...?" I asked, raising an eyebrow.

"No, quite the opposite," Hagerty insisted. "It was a platonic friendship between like-minded, active boys. When Jimmy was 13, he was either seduced or raped by the Catholic priest whom he assisted at Mass. Jimmy hung himself soon after, and Gavin was never able to forgive a Church that hushed up so many similar scandals."

"Could that trauma have played a role in Gavin's alcoholism?" I asked.

"Probably," he shrugged, "but there are genetic factors too. From what he told me, Gavin was not the first Owen to balance his scales with the demon whiskey."

"Did he mention anything else that bothered him?" I asked.

"He was never specific," Hagerty replied. "But he did tell me he got involved in something in his early twenties that he had mixed feelings about. It led to both great good and great evil, in his estimation. He also said that that when you stick your foot in the river of history, there's no telling what will bite it off."

"Hmm," I said noncommittally, and showed him Owen's last poem.

"What do you make of this?" I asked.

Hagerty smoothed out the creases with a clinical hand and frowned.

"It doesn't convey much to me. It seems packed with meaning, yet opaque." I nodded.

"Have you tried googling it?", he asked. "Some stanzas of the poem, I mean? I used to paste in paragraphs of student essays when I taught university, and too often I'd find they stole the text from some site."

My jaw dropped. I hate the way that phrase has been appropriated by "jaw dropping" ad copywriters. But there actually was a perceptible gap between my lips for an instant. Of course, search engines match keywords to sites that contain the maximum number of instances of them, so if I pasted a lot of the poem into the search bar, I might get something.

"If he were to hide some, say, evidence of what he'd gotten into, where would you look?"

"Maybe," he continued thoughtfully, "Gavin's bird houses."

"I didn't see any around the house," I said.

"You wouldn't," Hagerty replied. "He built them in his basement workshop, and the door's hard to find." Time to turn my detecting up a notch, I thought.

"But he would only put them in the woods behind his place. He felt that it was vulgar for beings as beautiful as birds to have to beg at human houses for food."

"Perhaps he put something in one of them," I said, remembering "These are not quite last words, Leave we those to the birds."

"It's a possibility," he agreed.

We chatted a few minutes more. I enjoyed Hagerty's agile mind, obviously not in retirement mode yet despite his age. But he knew little else useful to me.

"One last question. Do you think he was murdered?" I asked, on my way out.

He paused. "I wouldn't discount it. Gavin described himself as paranoid, but he said that even paranoids can have someone after them. He seemed more worried than usual the last few times I saw him. If he really took part in something dangerous long ago, maybe it came back to haunt him."

We shook hands and I wound my bike back along the same road, feeling the front end lift as the motor howled. When I throttled back, it was so quiet that, except for my exhaust and the onrushing wind, all I heard was the discordant, taxi-driver-protest of a big echelon of Canada geese flying south.

Back at Owen's house, I made myself a quick lunch – his larder majored in canned tuna and ham, mayo, and frozen loaves of bread, so I concocted a sandwich. The only remotely healthy addition was a handful of chives I plucked from his ragged herb garden.

I started his computer up again and, when the password watchdog appeared, I typed in "Jimmy." Bingo. I now had access to his document files. But a quick skim-and-scan revealed little except drafts of letters to the editor over outrages varying from Papal arrogance to the scattering of bio-solid sludge (which Owen preferred to call "shite") over Prince Edward County's farm fields. There were many literary files as well – poems that died aborning, random notes and fragmentary chapters for a new novel.

He also appeared – probably fortuitously – to have abandoned a nonfiction effort, a literary study of farting with the working title "FlatuLit". There were notes including a scientific explanation of why farting was essential to the human digestive system. Otherwise, we'd explode from the methane produced during food absorption. There was an analysis of all farts into four main categories: open (e.g. loud); closed, AKA squeakers, in which tension in the sphincter produced resonances less musical than those from trumpets and tubas; periodic, in which a chain of small explosions issued, especially when the farter was walking; and silent. My schoolmates called this variety SBD (silent but deadly) and our best proponent of the art was Hughie Ellis, who could from an open classroom window kill passing birds with his salutes. Or so he claimed.

Other research detailed the farting comedian of classical Rome celebrated in Fellini's *Satyricon*, and a citation from Joyce's *Ulysses*: "the salute of Almidano Artifoni's sturdy trousers swallowed by a closing door." There was even a royal angle: The Earl of Oxford, Edward de Vere, when making a bow to Queen Elizabeth I, let one rip. Feeling shamed, he undertook a voluntary exile of seven years. Finally, the Queen welcomed him back with, "My Lord, I had forgotten the fart."

OK, that was more about the subject than I really wanted to know. Had he finished the book, it probably wouldn't be challenging the Harry Potter novels for sales.

His email in-box proved more fruitful. I ignored messages from fans, literary researchers, and spammers promising everything from "genuine replica watches" to faithful Russian brides, discount Cialis and hidden fortunes in Africa. Some of them, in an attempt to defeat anti-spam blockers by sounding like a real message, quoted random strings of text, including a long passage from Dickens. I wonder how the great Victorian storyteller would have felt about his beautifully punctuated and cadenced prose helping to sell more reliable erections.

What caught my eye were a couple of terse messages titled simply WARNING. The "from" address was un-illuminating: anon49013@petet.fin. When I clicked to expand the header and find the path of the message, I realized the email was routed through one of those anonymous, origin-hiding email forwarding services beloved of criminals, terrorists, and child-porn addicts.

The messages themselves were not very informative, but clear in intent.

"Keep your mouth shut, old man, or we'll make an open-and-shut case of you," read the latest one.

"Remember your oath. You can't change what was done, and it's better the world never knows for sure," the previous one said, a little more gently.

I couldn't find any replies to these. If Owen had responded, he'd erased his sent mail. I wasn't enough of a hacker to dredge up erased messages.

Then I remembered Hagerty's suggestion and typed in a few stanzas of the poem Owen had left. I was surprised that the search bar actually took it all.

I swore softly, as site after site filled the screen, most pointing to the same thing: JFK's assassination, the mother of more conspiracy theories, ranging from plausible to crack-brained, than anything else in the 20th century. Except maybe the international banking system.

I realized why, as I opened the first hit in a list of several thousand. Lee Harvey Oswald (Oz?) had told the police he was a "patsy" for the murder before Jack Ruby shot him. What had previously escaped my notice was a recent development: a *Rolling Stone* article detailing the confessions of long-time CIA operative E. Howard Hunt, who, if one believed the deathbed words dictated to his son, was involved in something more significant than Watergate. Could he be the "hunt" alluded to in Gavin's doggerel, who found no prey? E. Howard claimed to have been on the fringes of a large-scale plot to kill Kennedy; the CIA had turned the job of whacking JFK over to the Mafia, who had their own reasons to hate him.

They had lost millions when Castro nationalized their casinos and other assets and were not amused when Kennedy failed to provide enough military support for the Bay of Pigs invasion. According to Hunt, his own role was as a "bench warmer." But Mafia figures in Florida, Louisiana and Chicago had subcontracted the job to associates in the Corsican outfit, who at the time were moving heroin to North American and European markets. One of the Corsicans, reputedly the long-rumoured gunman on the grassy knoll, Hunt named as Lucien Sarti, a stone killer supposedly shot to death a few years later in Mexico.

Hmm, multiple bells were ringing here as the Jabberwocky-like fog around the poem began to clear: "There was the non-Bouchard butcher/ The last word in non-existentialism..." That probably pointed to Sarti (Sartre) as well as digging at the one-legged former separatist premier of Quebec, whose name means "butcher" *en Anglais.*

Another site: "It was claimed by the journalist, that Guerini organized the assassination of President Kennedy. According to his contact, Christian David, the killing was carried out by Sarti and two other members of the Marseilles mob."

Plus, the "almighty head-state schism" must mean poor Kennedy's skull, which as the Zapruder film made only too clear, had exploded from the last shot. That was the kill shot; if Sarti had fired it rather than Oswald, this would explain the line about packing "more punch than the patsy." Could Owen have hated Catholics so much that he actually helped kill Kennedy, the US's first-ever RC President?

I sat on the couch, stunned. If Owen actually was involved, or added proof to Hunt's allegations, there was no way to keep a lid on this for long. Every conspiracy connoisseur and journalist in the world would chase this story. It also provided a dandy motive for killing Owen. A long list of witnesses and people peripherally related to Kennedy and his assassination had met untimely and/or violent ends. Consider Mary Meyer, whom the Hunt article mentioned. One of Kennedy's many lovers, she was married to CIA agent Cord Meyer, another man with no reason to love Kennedy. She made panicked phone calls to friends about a cover-up of the assassination. Her murder, which followed in a few days, was never solved.

The nocturnal visits of my balaclava-clad acquaintance made sense, too. Whether or not he had pulled the trigger on Owen, he was probably, like the Watergate janitors, sent to clean up embarrassing traces.

This was staggering stuff: exciting; dangerous; even historic. So far, though, nothing firm tied Owen to the actual assassination. Without new evidence, this would be at most one more thread in the endless weaving of theorists that included Oliver Stone, Jim Garrison, and now Hunt. Maybe Hunt knew the truth; maybe he was just spinning one more lure for the liberal media to gulp.

Still, my luck was running today – I was two-for-two on cracking Owen's password and decoding the poem. If fortune comes in threes, it was time to go birdhouse watching. I put on my motorcycle jacket and boots, and headed toward the tree line at the rear of the property. Approaching the first large trees, a mix of maples, beeches, birches, with the odd pine thrown in, I ducked to inspect a colourful mushroom and was startled to hear something whiz overhead. A chunk of bark flew off the nearest maple, accompanied by a ricochet sound.

I had heard no shot – the sniper must have been using a silencer – but that didn't slow my headfirst dive behind the tree. I wondered, absently, if this was the same gun and shooter combination that had done in Gavin. I speculated, less absently, whether I was going to die here. Would my obituary recall, ironically, someone's line about "the only thing that can kill a minor poet is a misprint"? Not that I thought I was minor, necessarily, but that's where the current crop of critics and anthologists had relegated me. *Focus, Miles.*

Why was I worrying about my literary reputation when someone was trying to kill me? I tried the old Western movie trick of brandishing an item of clothing. I picked my jacket for its bright colour, and waved it on a stick to draw more fire. Nothing. I listened in the autumnal silence, hearing the breeze rattling drying leaves on the branches and then the distant sound of a car driving away. The son of a bitch had probably propped his rifle on the side window sill and used it as a firing rest.

I considered my options. I could go home and change my underwear or give up the whole thing and just lie here until someone found my cowering corpse. I could get on with the job I'd been paid for. Much as I hate to be task-oriented (something few employers would accuse me of), I chose door number three.

I found a few birdhouses easily. They were brightly painted in tones of red, blue and yellow and well made, showing nice joinery. Owen must have been sober when he finished them. I hadn't seriously climbed a tree since my teens, but fortunately there were enough low branches to help me check out each house. None of them held anything more suspicious than empty nests, although one preserved melancholy blue-green eggs which had never hatched for some reason. *Pesticides?* I wondered glumly. By now, I was nearly at the other fringe of this woodlot. Occasional traffic crunched along the gravel road.

I had checked out four birdhouses. As I gazed idly around, I could see no more primary splashes of colour. Discouraged, I began to walk back to the house, but then my eye caught a strand of blue plastic waving high up in a pine. I saw it was tied to a birdhouse that looked different; unpainted, it had weathered to a silvery brown close to the hue of the tree trunk. Had it not been for the blue strand, I would never have noticed it.

I climbed the tree with some effort, pungent needles sticking into me, gummy sap adhering to my hands. I could just get my hand in the entry hole. Half-expecting to be pecked by an angry bird, I found instead a zip-loc bag holding a small brown envelope, its flap glued shut.

Panting slightly, I regained the ground. I'd have to add working out more often to my ever-growing list of good intentions.

Inside was a small chrome key and a note that read Corn Maze: Usury 417.

Great. So nice of Owen to bequeath me transparent instructions. He could have left a note explaining clearly where all the evidence he had secreted was. But I was beginning to recognize his style; the man thought not in straight lines, but in convoluted loops. Anyone following his footsteps would have to do the same.

I had no problem with the words themselves: "usury" is a nice, if archaic term, for loaning of money at excessive interest rates, and could be found any number of times in the works of Ezra Pound. But "corn maze"? Could he have misspelled "maize," and even if he had, what was I supposed to do? Dig up all the nearby corn fields? Or only the ones with 417 stalks in them?

Maybe Gavin only meant that a loaned bottle of 41.7 per cent alcohol corn liquor was amazing.

Chapter Five

Carefully replacing key and note in the envelope and tucking it into an inside pocket, I walked back with the tingling feeling between the shoulder blades inspired by being shot at. Hitting the computer again, I searched "Prince Edward County" and "corn maze", and damned if there wasn't one, next to a big barn turned into a concert hall on the fringes of a town named Wellington. The website revealed this town to be a long, pretty community spread along the waterway that allows boaters to leave West Lake and enter Lake Ontario proper. Did it have a bank, I wondered. It seemed to have no pawnbrokers or payday loan companies, the usual suspects for "usury."

Yes, it had a bank. It was open for a whole 30 minutes longer. I checked my watch, started my bike, and broke speed limits on the way to Wellington. I cleverly bypassed Picton, the de facto county capital, by checking the road map I'd taped to my gas tank. I kept a close watch in my mirrors for a nondescript sedan with a dimple-chinned driver, but nothing set off my alarms.

I made it to the bank with minutes to spare and a few bugs in my teeth – the sign of a happy rider. The bank manager, a conservative-looking matron, was dubious at first, but when I showed her the letter and encouraged her to call Gavin's cell phone, she agreed to take me to safe deposit box 417. Since I was not an executor, she would list what was in the box and make sure I left everything there.

After we went through the two-key unlocking routine, we found a white envelope with some cash in mixed currencies – US, British, Swiss – a couple of gold coins, and a manila envelope. I handed her the money and opened the envelope.

What I saw inside made me exclaim involuntarily: "Oh, shit." The manager glared, but I ignored her. Here was what looked to be a typed account of Gavin Owen's adventures in and around Texas in the fall of 1963, and a black-and-white glossy photograph of a much younger Owen. He stood beside a beetle-browed, swarthy guy brandishing an unusual-looking rifle with a telescopic sight.

I carefully recorded each typed page and the photograph with my digital camera. Mindful of the bank manager's tapping foot, I was about to return the contents to the box when I flipped the photo over. There, in browning ink on the back, was an inscription: "Lucien et Gavin, les deux mosquetaires. Merde aux tirants!" My French was good enough to know that whoever wrote this couldn't spell, but maybe that wasn't his chief talent.

I headed back chez Owen, my thoughts tumbling as if in a dryer. It was beginning to seem that, for the investment of a gallon of gas and a day of my time, I now had a likely motive for Owen's murder. By rights, I should have been letting the police know all this. But I had no intention of doing so until I'd read those typed pages. Even with them as evidence, I could picture the reaction of the local constabulary. Once I tied Owen's death to the JFK assassination, they'd be checking my head for aluminum foil hats, and politely inquiring how my last abduction by aliens had gone.

They seemed dedicated officers so far, but I could imagine they'd prefer to write Owen's death off as a tragic accident rather than have their sleepy County transfixed by the glare of a thousand TV cameras.

I made some quick stops in Picton, picking up a few JFK assassination conspiracy books at a used bookstore, a bottle of local red wine, and a pay-as-you-go cell phone. Generally, I abhor cell phones. They seem designed to destroy the civilities of public space, as well as private reflection. There's nothing worse than being subjected to the loudly-declaimed half of someone's banal conversation. The one I'd left in Toronto I kept only for business, and even so, I was often tempted to cast it into the Don River.

This thought recalled my great-uncle Gregory, who had finally given into his wife's and neighbours' urging and invested in a telephone for his country house. But he never phoned anyone, and callers bothered him with needless chitchat and sales offers, so he told the phone company to take it back... just before the first bill, with its installation charge, arrived. According to his scandalized wife, Gregory had chopped the phone into bite-size pieces with his firewood axe and mailed the remains in a box back to Bell, probably with a note saying "Heres yr phone. Dont call me abot it."

The sun was sinking, flooding the sky with those beautiful pastel pinks and oranges that only come with mid-autumn. Soon the sky was dark except for a rim of muted tangerine crowning a black line of bare trees.

I parked my bike at the back of the house again, figured out how to connect my camera to the house computer and download my images, and then I managed to get images of the typed pages grinding out of Owen's old printer. Some days I am a genius. Make that some moments.

Then I found the entrance to the basement, at the back of a closet. The door was well-concealed, with clothes hooks and assorted coats hanging on it. When I pulled it open, I saw rough-hewn steps. The basement also had a door to the outside, which I pried open and cleared of the junk resting against it. I oiled its hinges and left it ajar. The musty cellar held a well-appointed workshop, with high-end Makita woodworking tools... and a few other things I could use: a couple of rolls of foam, a sleeping bag still in its original box, even a dark fright wig that Owen must have bought for a disguise. Or a drunken Hallowe'en party.

I carried my findings back upstairs, and cooked up a gourmet cheddar and macaroni dinner from a box, using slightly sour milk from the fridge. Testing the limits of my cooking ability, I softened a frozen bag of peas with a few shots from a hammer, and tossed the remnants into a pot of boiling water. Three major food groups for dinner, if you consider that orange powdered stuff cheese.

Checking that the last page had spit out of the printer, I set to work with my basement finds and some purloined bedding from upstairs. I soon had constructed a simulacrum of a sleeping man on the coach, back turned to the window the burglar had used.

I watched part of one of my favourite cult films: *Repo Man*, with the great Harry Dean Stanton turning in one of his patented world-weary performances, and the car trunk's glowing radiation. It was on Gavin's shelf next to a DVD titled *Roman Catholicism's Most Secret Rites*, which I didn't sample. I made myself a bed in the basement, turned off lights upstairs until only one small lamp lit the living room, and went downstairs with my cell phone and motorcycle gear. I had also decorated the window with a string of dental floss, weighted with a suspended assortment of keys and kitchen spoons.

All these procedures were just my way of building up anticipation, which the wise say is the larger part of pleasure. Finally, I felt ready to read the pages Owen had secreted in the bank, but obviously couldn't bring himself to destroy.

ONE AUTUMN IN THE SOUTH: A MEMOIR

It's difficult to descry how the future will remember one. For me, there are a number of possibilities. It might be that novel, *Felt Life Grow*, which brought me money and fame, but also a lingering curse; has anything I've written since then met the same standard? It might be my poetry, should the pundits of 2050 AD (I refuse to use that politically correct code CE), find any importance in poetry at all, amid the whirring distraction of virtual worlds. Perhaps I will be recalled simply for outstanding curmudgeonliness and cantankerousness, or as the unknowing father of some bastard child who turns out to be more noteworthy than I.

Truly, it would be an irony of epic proportions if one event, neither sexual nor literary, in which I participated during my foolish youth becomes that solitary footnote carved into the granite face of time.

Whoever you are, gentle reader that found this memoir, I trust you have wit enough to savour the ironies in what I am about to relate. You were clever enough to follow the few cookie crumbs Hanselled for you.

Rewind to the early 1960's. I had an inheritance from a maiden aunt and little inclination to continue studies past my MA. I felt the need for lived experience. I was in possession not only of a then-respectable sum, but also a '57 Chevy whose sharp-finned lines would fetch a good price at one of those dreadfully necrophiliac vintage car auctions today. Where would I go to add to the knowledge and memories that someday, I vowed, would turn into a meaningful book or two? I would trace the footsteps of the writer I most venerated then: William Faulkner, the Nobel Laureate of Oxford, Mississippi. Faulkner understood, as did few writers, the way that history, family and community warp the growth of a person, giving him a sense of place in the universe, yet restricting his freedom to imagine and become.

In the steamy South, I thought I might find other roadside attractions; a wider and more complaisant variety of women than the knees-welded virgins who infested Ontario then, and perhaps some edifying conversation with those white-hooded Klan gentlemen of the south who shared my hatred of Popery. I am no racist, mind you. Some of the finest minds I've admired have lived under skins far from white in hue, and I thought lynching an excessive form of criticism (I'm adapting a jest here).

Some of my peers, inflamed by the ill-disciplined prose of Jack Kerouac, hit the road for thumb-powered jaunts across the USA. That was not my choice; I planned to stay in modest comfort at motels and tourist cabins, driving myself rather than trusting to the whim of hitchhikers' unpredictable, sometimes pederast, hosts.

After wending my way through Mississippi and a few erotic experiences too wonderful to spoil with prose, I found myself in New Orleans. Here, in the wonderfully-yclept Pirates Alley, Faulkner had written his first novel, *Soldiers' Pay*. This was far from his best, but we all have to start somewhere. New Orleans was a wonderful city then, at once mouldering and vital, historic and careless. I liked its Dixieland jazz companies, the un-Ontario ease of wandering along a street with a beer in my hand, the cemeteries with their crypts elevated in case of flooding, Marie Laveau's voodoo shop of dark objects. It has always struck me how mostly Catholic cities have active sindustries: strip clubs, speakeasies, bordellos and gambling dens.

Perhaps there is little point in going to confession unless you've worked up a few whoppers to retail to your shocked-but-secretly-titillated auditor, so you can wipe the moral slate clean and start sinning all over again. The next time I belabour a priest about the head, I must verify this with him!

Needless to say, I took full advantage of these businesses, as well as of local ladies, whose delightfully easygoing attitude about sex was animated by their voluptuous, magnolia-scented bodies in every shade of skin from lily white to espresso. Understand, I am not boasting; any reasonably presentable man with morals as loose as his purse strings would have done well there. I am simply establishing the context for my fateful meeting late that October with a mysterious man known only to me as Mike. I doubt that was his true name.

Many of the men I had casual converse with in my swing through the South were unsophisticated, unaware of much of their own culture, let alone the rest of the world's. Mike was different. He spotted my dog-eared copy of *The Sound and the Fury* beside my tumbler of bourbon in a French Quarter dive, and we started talking books. He actually had read a few.

His knowledge of the greater world surpassed mine; I gathered he had been a mercenary in hot spots in Indochina and newly decolonized Africa. However, he politely refrained from giving too many details, adding with an easy grin that he could leave me among the living that way.

Discovering that I was Canadian, he asked my outsider's opinion of John Fitzgerald Kennedy, the first Roman Catholic and youngest president-elect ever at that point.

"I admire his adventuresome taste in ladies, although Jackie's a bit of a stick figure for my tastes," I said. "However, and I hope sincerely you're not Catholic, I'd never trust any son of a bitch vassal of the Pope to run a major nation with nuclear arms."

Mike reached over and gave my right hand a bone-shredding shake. "Damned if I and a lot of people don't agree with you," Mike said. He sounded me out about my views on many topics for the rest of that long and drunken evening. I had the sense that this was some kind of interview, with no idea what I'd applied for. He even asked to see my passport, on the pretext that despite his travels, he'd never seen a Canadian one before. I happened to have brought it in case I decided on a quick trip to Mexico. I thought his request curious, but showed him anyway, and he looked carefully through it.

After dropping me off at my hotel, Mike promised to pick me up the next day for a jaunt to Texas. I was too inebriated and tired to wonder why.

The next day around noon, he showed up, true to his word. We had the obligatory *café au lait* and powdered beignets at Café du Monde. I checked out of my hotel, and followed Mike to a suburban street, where he carefully locked up his car in an anonymous-looking garage.

Following his directions, we set off in my Chevrolet for a ranch in Texas. Its location I will not name, save to say it was not all that far from Dallas. Mike was a good travelling companion – not tiresomely loquacious, but capable of amusing observations about the sites and sights we passed. When we arrived at the ranch, Mike introduced me to a varied and engaging bunch of cutthroats: Sicilian mobsters from the US, their Corsican brothers from France, and some disaffected veterans of the CIA and the previous year's Bay of Pigs debacle. They were so different from the writers and academics I had usually associated with that they almost seemed another species. They acted without regret or even thought, sometimes: creatures of impulse and reflex. Yet they were loyal to their beliefs and fellows, however distasteful these might be to mainstream society.

Most of them came and went, but I stayed on, sensing that something potentially significant was being cooked up here. I befriended one of the Corsicans in particular, a thug introduced to me as Lucien. "I was born Catholic," he apologized to me, having heard of my animus for that cursed religion. I forget whether he spoke in English or French, as both dialects were heavily accented by his native island's vernacular. "But I choose now to send others to heaven, in the sure hope of going to Hell myself." It was only upon my eventual parting with this man that I learned his surname: Sarti.

After I was subjected to a few tests of nerve, commitment, and hatred of the Kennedy dynasty, I was called before a committee of these violent men one night. Lucien produced a stiletto, drew a line of blood across my palm and then his, clasped our hands together and made an announcement. "We have come to a crossroads," he said to me. "You may leave now without learning our true purpose, although some day you may hear about it. If you stay, we will give you a small part in our drama. I will treat you as a blood brother. But if you ever betray the cause, or any of us," he flicked the stiletto to my throat, "I and every other man in this room will hunt you down and kill you."

This was so ridiculously melodramatic that I half-expected to see a camera crew in one corner with the director signalling for more blood, and a Mafia "advisor" rolling his eyes. However, I read from the countenances of Lucien and the others that they took this neo-medieval ritual very seriously.

What could I say? Here was experience of a rawer kind than I had expected.

I took their oath and set myself on the road to being an eyewitness and male handmaiden to the death of America's elected leader, loved by the public but despised by many powerful groups in his country.

Like any good terrorist cadre, we were just one cell in the overall plan. I was told a little of what was being planned. When Kennedy toured through Dallas, he would receive a warm welcome from three gunmen, staked out in carefully triangulated locations. Lucien was to be positioned with an almost head-on shot at the presidential vehicle. Another Corsican, who was with us on the ranch, would be on the second floor of an office building, firing almost horizontally from behind the car, and the third sniper (who I never met) would be positioned on the sixth floor of an ugly edifice called the Texas Schoolbook Depository.

My role was nothing as dramatic as pulling a trigger. Instead, I was to accompany and provide cover for Lucien, who would be dressed as a Dallas police officer. After the shooting, I would drive him away in my car while he changed outfits. With Canadian plates and my curious Northern twang, I could enact the Nicely Confused Tourist, and Lucien (with yet another of his forged passports) would play my linguistically challenged cousin from Quebec.

We rehearsed the critical part of our mission many times. I was to stand beside him while he assembled the custom-made sniper rifle. If anyone showed undue interest in us, I would warn him.

Once he had fired the necessary shot(s), the rifle broke down into two sections: the barrel, bolt, silencer, trigger assembly and telescopic sight constituted one; the stock and receiver another. Each of us would conceal our part in cleverly-designed webbing that hung down our backs. As long as we stood straight, the rifle parts were invisible under a loose jacket or coat.

As I am no fool, it entered my mind that all this planning must have been orchestrated by men with wealth, power and connections, not to mention intelligence. It was no easy task managing the logistics of a group that included me, the Corsicans, American gangsters, CIA operatives, Cuban exiles, and God knows who else. But I was never told who was pulling the strings, and I realized that this sort of knowledge that could lead to my untimely demise. It did for many others, in the years following the assassination.

Fear, anticipation and doubt filled me. But I could not show my wavering to resolute men like Lucien, and when the fateful day came, I played my part well enough. The day itself was almost anti-climactic. I would not appreciate the true gravity of what I had been part of until the newscasts, inquiries, and obsessive reviewing of amateur films and snapshots that followed the assassination. I parked my car just a block away. We had to change our site from the planned bridge when we found a couple of real police officers guarding it. Despite Lucien's convincing uniform, I didn't think anyone would mistake his English for a Texan drawl.

Instead, we stood just behind a picket fence on a grassy knoll and waited. Scattered clumps of people lined the streets and the fronts of the office buildings of Dealey Plaza. A few stood below us on the knoll, backs turned to us, and a young Negro couple sat some distance away on a wall, sharing a fast-food lunch. But no-one paid us any attention.

The motorcade crept into view and turned the corner, heading almost directly toward us. When the first shot came from the Textbook Building, few immediately noticed it, although a few turned or pointed to the sixth-floor window. We were waiting for this signal. Lucien raised the rifle to his shoulder, sighted and waited for one more shot, which came soon. No one looked towards us – all eyes were on the motorcade.

We saw Governor Connally jerk as if he'd been hit. Onlookers began screaming and throwing themselves to the ground, finally realizing what was happening. Lucien, cool as ever, fired and was rewarded by the sight of the President's head exploding. "C'est fini," he said matter-of-factly. He lowered the rifle and broke it into its components. Each of us hid our share and then slowly walked away from the scene. The motorcade accelerated away with its sacrificial victim, and we returned to my car and drove away without anyone questioning us.

We met some of the other conspirators back at a safe house in suburban Dallas. Whoever was pulling our strings had wisely decided that minimal exposure to the public and police was the safest policy for the next week or so. We ate barbecue, slapped each other's backs, and watched in fascination as the television reporters breathlessly informed us of the President's death, the quick (and probably illegal) removal of his body from Dallas police control to Washington, the inauguration of Johnson, who I thought did not look quite as downcast as he should, and the arrest and subsequent shooting of Oswald. When we saw the footage of Ruby executing Oswald, one of the mobsters gloated: "At last – they took the pawn."

Lucien posed for and inscribed the back of a photo taken with me, he proudly displaying the fatal rifle. Then he gave me as a memento the spent cartridge that had killed Kennedy, and a second round he had not needed to fire. He flew to Detroit and from there, perhaps, to Montreal. I never saw him again. I made my own way back to Canada, and avoided telling anyone where I'd been on November 22, or what I done then. Everyone else seemed to remember. That day became a event that seared itself into recollections.

Since then, I have sometimes wondered about the wisdom of our action.

I have few regrets about ridding the world's most powerful country of a leader who – despite his protestations of a nonsectarian Presidency – would have danced to the Piper Pope. But I wonder if the various Protestants who succeeded him were really any better.

Kennedy, despite his brinkmanship over the Cuba Missile Crisis, did not have his heart set on war-mongering the way many of his successors, including the basset-faced Johnson, did. Would letting him live have saved innocent souls around the world? Maybe. On the other hand, the conspiracy's machinations probably would have rolled on without my participation. So this is all moot, shite under the bridge.

I have watched with considerable amusement the fumbling attempts of first the Warren Commission, next the United States House Select Committee on Assassinations, and then many books, articles and even that tiresome Oliver Stone movie to make sense of the best-documented assassination ever. There was no shortage of evidence; what it all meant turned out to be anyone's guess. It would require, I hate to say, almost Jesuitical reasoning. I have kept my pact with Lucien and the others until now. So have the rest, and in most cases death has long saved them the necessity of voluntary silence.

Whether I was right or wrong to play my modest role, I will let history judge. Just know this: I was there. You may question my motives in breaking a vow of silence I have kept so long. I have already questioned the effect it may have on my place in history, but we will let Clio decide that.

There is one other reason to finally make the truth known: imagine all the energy, time and money that have gone into unraveling the tangled threads of this assassination. Both scholars and crackpots have invested much in attempting to decode Kennedy's death. Perhaps now all those resources can be turned to a better end: detailing the sins of the Roman Cardinals and Popes: the Spanish Inquisition, complicity in the Holocaust, the impoverishing of the devout poor everywhere to line the coffers of the Church and its often obese priests, the litany of child abuse.

If you require harder evidence of my account, let me offer an alliterative clue: visit the vehement vintner where the rabbit ran.

Chapter Six

Well, that *was* quite a story. I sat staring at the wall, stunned. Although it fitted with what I had read about the assassination and some of the countless bits of often-contradictory evidence, I had my doubts. Owen could have been there and done what he claimed. Or he could, with his novelist's skills, have concocted a story that fit the facts as known, buttressed with some picture of him with a random hunter from anywhere. I could picture him chuckling in the afterlife, as he sent me on the wild goose chase to end all wild goose chases. There were certainly hints of the same tricksterism in E. Howard Hunt's account, in which he claimed to have been one of several operatives impersonating tramps to give conflicting evidence to the investigators.

I would have to do some more investigation before I bought his tale, not only because it had the greatest news potential of anything since 9/11, but also because I owed it to my clients. I rolled the pages up carefully, and taped a dark plastic bag around them. Then I stored them in my bike – not in the obvious saddlebags, but in a hidden recess designed to hold a long-gone safety chain for locking the wheels.

Tomorrow, I'd better let Richard know what I'd found. I made my bed in the basement and prepared to sleep in it.

I was about to doze off, when I heard what I'd been waiting for... an engine shutting off suddenly; gravel crunching; silence. Then the window going up again. It was all so déjà vu again until the jangle of the keys and spoons, and the intruder's expletive. Next I heard two muffled thumps, exactly like someone firing silenced rounds into the sleeping non-me on the couch.

Then I heard voices; the perp must have brought a partner.

I listened for a moment, and heard one call the other "Hank." I dialed 9-1-1 and quietly reported the third break-in in three nights at the same location – a trifecta, probably a county record. Then I crept out the back door with my motorcycle boots, helmet, and jacket, which I quickly donned.

I watched through the rear window as the furtive pair flicked their flashlights around. They stripped the blankets off the dummy and kicked it to pieces. One of them opened the computer case and waved what looked like a large magnet over the hard drive a few times.

I heard the police siren about the same time they did. This time they didn't bother with the window, kicking open the front door and piling into their car. The siren sounded only about a minute away, but I was tired of having my sleep disturbed. I wanted these guys.

I waited until I heard their motor start, and then pulled on my helmet and got my bike going. I had once installed a switch that cut out the headlight and taillight circuits. They're supposed to be always on in Ontario, but there are times when a biker's delicate sensibilities prefer darkness. This was one of them. I gave them a small lead, and then revved up in pursuit. It was no contest. My bike may be 25 years old, but it still accelerates at a rate that only an exotic sports car can match. American sedans are no contest.

I stayed behind them around a couple of curves, and then we came up to a sharp right-hand turn through another mini-forest. They hadn't seen me yet, but the reflection of my brake light on the trees must have shown in their rear-view mirror or something, because I saw a flash from the passenger side, and a bullet took off my right-side mirror. Damn. Those are hard to replace. I'd have to go onto eBay. I hunched over my handlebars, and saw another tight turn coming up, this one to the left. Timing it carefully, I gunned the engine, cut to the left, and with a rather balletic kick, if I do say so myself, I swung my steel-toed right boot through the driver's side window.

Startled, he swerved the car to the right, and I was rewarded with the thunk of a car hitting one of the solid old County trees that had accounted for many unwary drivers,. The car's airbags inflated.

I failed to control the wobble that my kick had initiated. The bike crashed as I attempted to balance it, and the motor stopped. Although I wasn't much hurt, I was embarrassed. I limped over to the crashed car. The passenger was the thug from the night before, his arm hanging limply out the window, a pistol on the ground below. I couldn't really see the driver because of the airbag, but he wasn't moving either. I took the gun, and fired it into two of the tires in case anyone tried to drive the wreck away.

I reached for my brand-new cell phone, and then realized I had left it behind in the rush to chase the car. I frisked the passenger, but he was phoneless as well. So I walked along the road for ten minutes until a friendly farmer in a rusty pickup stopped and asked what the heck I was doing strolling along a county road in the night. Was I one a them fool tourists who didn't know no better? Didn't I know there was man-eating coyotes at every turn? I convinced him to take me to the headquarters of Prince Edward County's finest. He dropped me near the station, noting that he hadn't exactly got around to keeping up his license, insurance, and DriveClean status. I shook his hand anyway.

This time I was lucky. Constable Lemieux was on duty with a male partner, not the cop from the night before. I explained what had happened, gave them the pistol I had confiscated from the car, and led them back to the wreck.

The airbags had deflated. The passenger wasn't going anywhere; his throat was cut, giving him a sickening second mouth. The cops looked at me, but I shook my head and held my hands up, proclaiming innocence. I felt ill; should I have pulled them out of the wreck? Stayed there? But I had no reason to believe that one would terminate the other. My story was helped by the fact that the driver was nowhere to be found; neither was the knife.

As her partner noted the details, Constable Lemieux surveyed me with her hands on her hips. I noted that they were nice hips. "Two break-ins, firearms discharged, a car and motorcycle crash, a murder... and you've barely been here twenty-four hours. According to you. Are things always this exciting when you show up?" she asked.

"Rarely," I said. "I'm normally a quiet, retiring poet, turning out odes to lost love…" She snorted.

"Do you have any clue what all this is about?" she asked me.

"I have several clues," I replied. "But you're not going to like where they lead."

"Try me," she responded. I could see we were in for a long night. We had to wait for the ambulance to pick up the deceased and a tow truck to haul away the wreck. The quiet woods turned into a carnival of flashing red and yellow lights and crackling radios. The officers called in an APB on the driver, but unfortunately I had only seen him fleetingly through the house's window, and then half-covered in an airbag. There were good odds that he had at least superficial cuts and bruises on his face from my kicking in the window and then his crashing into the tree. Maybe a couple of nice air-bag-blackened eyes.

I found, with the aid of a borrowed OPP flashlight, that the crash had dislodged one of the cables from my bike's battery. I reconnected it, hit the starter, and my trusty steed appeared to be back in operating mode despite a few new dings.

The constable and her partner were about to go off shift. I suggested she and I meet on neutral ground. I've been in enough police stations to know that what is said in their public areas becomes everybody's business. Neutral ground turned out to be a pseudo-English pub. But the pale ale tasted good, the live country music was over, and the place had only half-a-dozen tables occupied, so we were able to secrete ourselves in a corner.

"To those who serve and protect," I toasted Constable Lemieux.

"And to the police, too," she said with a wink. She had wonderful green eyes.

"Umm… before we get into this, is there anything I can call you besides Constable?"

"Well, my given name I've never been totally happy with. It's Maryse. You can call me Mar, like "mare"— but no horse jokes, though."

I saluted her gravely.

"Did you come to the County to do more than clean up

Owen's house?" she asked.

"Yes," I said. "I have to protect client confidentiality, what's left of it, but let's just say his family had no reason to believe he was murdered. Someone had to look out for family interests in the aftermath of his death."

"And maybe keep wicked old Uncle Gavin from embarrassing them anymore?"

I couldn't answer, but I smiled and she let it go.

"Of course, it's your duty to investigate anything criminal you come across. However, before I show you something I've found, can you keep it quiet unless it proves to be material to a crime?" I asked.

"I'm good with that," she said, "but you're definitely whetting my curiosity."

I sighed, explained the twisted trail of clues that had led me to the safe deposit box in Wellington, and pulled the printed copy of Owen's memoir from my jacket.

"We have a deal," I said. "You read this and I'll drink."

She smoothed the pages out and read them in silence. She showed little reaction, but I could swear her dark eyebrows inched higher by the last page.

"For a poet, you seem fairly grounded," she said. "What do you think of all this?"

"I rather hope it's not true," I said. "I don't want a hundred conspiracy-crazed cranks beating down my door, and I can assure you the Owens don't either. But the details fit with some recent revelations about the assassination."

"Old Owen was certainly smart enough to dream this up, and make it sound plausible," she said. "But without him to swear to it, and no evidence beside an old Kodak print, it wouldn't exactly stand up in court. However, I'll get a warrant to remove the contents of the safe deposit box in case they are material to Owen's death."

I nodded. We each took a few swallows of dark amber ale.

"He could easily have paid someone with Photoshop skills to do a little work on an old photo of a couple of hunters, and merge his and Sarti's faces into it," I suggested. "As to whether that's an image of the real Lucien Sarti, it does look like him. I found a picture on a page that summed up that French journalist's interviews with Christian David."

"Do you think there's a tie-in with Owen's death, and the break-ins at his house?" she continued.

"I don't know. But so far I haven't found any other reason why someone would want to search his house and quite possibly kill him. On the other hand, the conspirators he mentions are probably all dead now. It's been 45 years since JFK died. Who would be hurt now if Owen's version turns out to be true?"

"Good question," she said. "Now what about the clue at the end of this... the vehement vintner?"

"I was hoping you'd solve that one," I said. "Where are the wineries around here?"

"Mostly near Wellington," she replied. "There's one on the fringe of Picton, and a few around Waupoos."

"Waupoos?" I repeated. "What a great name. Where's that?"

"It's on the southeast coast of the County, across from South Bay. And its name is a Native word that means...umm..."

She called to the bartender, a young man with long dark hair.

"Bruce from Waupoos, right?" she asked.

"Guilty," he said. "What'd I do?"

"Nothing I can prove," Mar answered. "What's the English meaning of Waupoos?"

"I think it's "rabbit"," he said.

"There you go," she said. "There's only three wineries I know of around there. Well, one of them mostly makes cider."

The bar was closing up, the last patrons easing out the door. I looked around and realized that Bruce, too polite to urge a member of the OPP out of his establishment, was waiting on us to finish. But she downed her pint and said she had to be back on duty in less than twelve hours.

"I'll check the wineries out tomorrow," I said.

"If we need to reach you for any reason..." she said. I gave her my new cell number.

We parted with a handshake. I rode back and returned to

my dank bed in the cellar. Despite Poe's great horror story "The Cask of Amontillado," I find them peaceful places, afterthoughts. Most of the action goes on above them. I didn't think the surviving burglar would be back that night, but one never knows. I found a working dehumidifier and turned it on. The white noise from its fan, the reassuring drip of extracted water into the holding tank, and my own comedown after all the adrenaline from the break-in and chase put me to sleep in no time.

Chapter Seven

The next day started with delicate wisps of fog over the fields and lower valleys, but it began to burn off once I was past Picton. I went by the collection of over 100 handmade birdhouses at Macaulay Mountain Conservation area, which looked worth a stop later, and accelerated out into open country. I turned off County Road 8, and soon wound my way down a long hill that led into Waupoos. This I earmarked as a fine bike road despite the winter piles of sand on some turns. There I passed another Ye Olde England-type pub, the Duke of something or other. Did you know that the Y in "Ye" is actually a rune called "thorn" and is pronounced as "th"? *Shut up, Miles, you're getting too holistic again.*

What a beautiful site the winery had, surrounded by vineyards and orchards sloping down to the bay. There was a high bush blueberry picking site with strung-up mesh screens keeping the birdies out. The people working the counter at the winery were friendly enough, so I ventured a taste of their wine and snapped up a bottle of the Baco Noir, which had a wonderfully smoky taste. None of them had heard of Gavin Owen, though, and my interrogation was interrupted by a whole busload of smiling Asian tourists led by a woman with a megaphone who managed to smile harder than the rest of them. "Irashaimas" she shrilled, welcoming them as if she were the proprietor instead of guide.

A short way along the road, past fragrant ripening apples, I cut a sharp left and revved up a steep short hill to the cider place. This had an even better view from its hill, with the lake sparkling in the distance like hammered silver, and a breeze blowing through the cidery doors.

This time I met the owner, a tall, sociable chap, confident in the quality of his cider. I had just a brief taste, to prove him right, since the PI Handbook frowns on heavy drinking before 11 a.m. I wouldn't have described him as "vehement," though, so I asked if he knew other winery owners who might fit that description.

"Well," he replied, waving away a yellow jacket circling his head, "the one that pops into my mind is Rod, who runs the place out toward Cressy. Look for his sign: Caves du Cressy Wine. He'll tell you before you ask that his wines are the only decent ones around here, and the rest of us should go back to making spruce beer."

I thanked him, and rode carefully back down the hill. Tourists and wine tasting are not always a motorcycle-friendly combination.

I couldn't see any such sign, though, although I enjoyed the bumpy, undulating road. The first person I passed was a woman with short, mauve-tinted hair, weeding her garden while wearing an incongruous pair of bright yellow latex gloves.

She looked up as I stopped politely at the edge of her driveway. I took off my helmet, and she said "Looking for me? If it's Moon Point Mary you want, you've found her."

"Actually, I'm looking for Rod at the winery," I said.

"What the hell for? Are you gay? If you just need a drink, I've got Chablis in the fridge."

She sighed histrionically when I explained that I only wanted Rod for information.

"The first dark, handsome stranger in days," she said, "and he just wants directions. Take off the 'dir' part, darlin', and I could help you out." She winked.

"Is it my imagination," I replied, "or are the women around here a little, well, flirtatious?"

She stuck her yellow-gloved hands on her hips, and stared at me. "Have you met the *men* around here? Thing is, when women get older, they get stronger and better, like a fine red. More who they are. The men just get older. Ol' Rod probably took his sign down when some tourist said the wrong thing about his Gamay and he had a hissy fit."

She told me to watch for a large, dying birch tree at the corner of a dirt lane back up the road. I thanked her and turned to ride away. When I looked in the rear-view mirror, I could have sworn she cupped her breasts at me and wagged her tongue. But when I swung my head around, she was back to weeding.

Sure enough, I found a curiously-painted wooden sign that announced the "Caves du Cressy Winery" lying flat in the grass beside a flaking birch tree. I followed a winding dirt road and then found a log building with huge glass windows.

A man who could only be Rod bustled out and asked me to turn off my motor.

"You know anything can disturb the vibrations of good wine when it's sleeping. And of course, we make the best there is in…"

Recognizing from the cidery owner's warning that this could stretch into an extended monologue, I cut him off. "Actually, I didn't come about wine," I said and handed him the by-now much-fingered letter from Richard.

He skimmed it, and then said, "I did know old Gavin. He was a drunk, but still had enough discrimination to tell me my merlot was the best red here."

"Did he leave anything with you?" I asked.

"Yes, he did…and I never knew what to make of it," he said. "Come in,"

He led me to the tasting counter, and rummaged through a drawer on the servers' side that was full of receipts and correspondence. "Here it is," he said. "Take this… I don't want it back. Gavin said it might bring me luck, but I think anything vibing of violence is bad for the vintages." At this, he smacked his hand down on a large fly crawling across the counter. This guy was too tightly wound to make restful wine, in my amateur opinion.

He handed me a match-box with a curious print of a pipe on it. Something inside the box rattled softly.

I thanked him, and waited until I was back on my bike before opening it. Inside was a tiny, sealed plastic bag holding a spent brass cartridge and unused bullet. The live round was a dum-dum, an X carefully incised in its blunt tip. Upon impact, the tip would mushroom, wreaking more havoc than a regular bullet.

I shook the opened box, and a fragment of yellow paper fell out. I bent over with some difficulty, realizing I should have got off my bike first, and retrieved the paper. On it was printed in tiny letters "Do not handle – check fingerprints. Spent round was the killer."

But what were the odds that any fingerprints would find a match? As far as I know, fingerprint records were deleted once their owners died, and Sarti was supposedly killed in Mexico over thirty years ago, victim of a plan to shift the world center of heroin exporting from the "French Connection" Corsican Mafia to the previous empire of the Aztecs.

I bought a padded envelope at a stationery store in Picton. Sealing the cartridge casing, bullet and note inside, I wrote a message to Mar, and left it for her at the OPP detachment. The clerk looked curiously at me, as if someone in biker regalia dropping off ammunition was not an everyday event. I resisted the urge to explain myself.

Back at the house, I made overdue phone calls. First, I updated Richard. I thought he should know that, given my recent experiences with shots, thugs, and break-ins, there were good odds that his uncle's death had not been an accident. He absorbed this in silence. Then he said, "He was a cranky old bastard. But he was our cranky old bastard, and had the right to live out his remaining years. Do you think the police will find his killer?"

"If they catch up with the driver of that car, maybe," I said. "Of course, the dead guy could have done the deed."

When I detailed the contents of the manuscript, he was concerned. "Is the original still safely locked away in the bank?" he asked.

I assured him that it was. "The JFK assassination!" he blurted. "Christ! That's all we need. If Uncle Gavin was involved, we'll never hear the end of it."

He told me to get the window repaired and bring the bill when I returned to Toronto.

I also called Sarah, reassured her that I was still alive, and gave her a somewhat edited version of my adventures. She tends to fret.

"There's one little thing you can help me with," I added. "Is there anyone out here in wherever I am now – central-eastern Ontario? South-eastern Ontario? – who's an authority on American history? Old Owen left a wild tale behind, and I'm not buying it without some more fact-checking. You know me, I need to understand the context."

"Context, schmontext. You're just trying to distract me from finding out if anyone ever checks out your poetry collections," she replied.

I could hear her fingers doing their demon dance on a keyboard. Another of my little PI secrets: if you really want to know something that's public information, ask a librarian. Most people view them as stampers of books and collectors of overdue fines, but they're trained to seek and evaluate information for others. Kind of like Poirots of the periodicals, Simenons of the stacks, Holmes of the... I was wool-gathering.

"Got you one," Sarah said, startling me. "Queen's University in Kingston.... Professor Dieter Friedrich is your man."

"A guy named that? Shouldn't he be named, oh, Buck Forbes or something? Oliver North?"

"Get a grip," she laughed. "Remember the Germanic Henry Kissinger? The Polish Zbigniew Kazimierz Brzezinski? American patriots, both of them."

She was showing off. But she had a right to. I thanked her and phoned Queen's. After an intriguing series of call transfers, I eventually ended up with Prof. Friedrich's administration person, who assured me the good professor would be in his office between 3:00 and 5:00 that afternoon for student hours.

"But I don't think you'll have to compete with many students," she added. "They have a major essay due and tend to stay away from him then."

Checking the map, I realized there were two ways to get there. The most direct way was to catch Highway 49 north, take the big bridge through the Mohawk reservation and Deseronto (sounded like "Desolate Toronto", somehow), and then follow the 401 East to Kingston. Or I could take the Glenora Ferry across the Bay of Quinte, wind my way past the Loyalists' first landing in these parts back in the 1700's, and then join the 401 further east.

What the hell. It was a beautiful sunny day, and I'd be expensing my gas. Besides, the map mentioned that the ferry dock was within a short detour of Lake on the Mountain, a curious, funnel-shaped body of very clear water whose surface was some seventy meters above the bay. Natives considered it a power site, the map added. I took a look at the lake, verifying that there was something uncanny about such quiet, limpid depths so close to a steep cliff. Then I blasted down the hill to catch the boat.

The ferry was fun, a tiny affair that took about a dozen cars and my bike on a less than ten-minute ride. Cormorants flapped overhead and gulls screamed the usual invective at our passage.

I hit Kingston in an hour, where I motored past the closed men's penitentiary, former home of Canada's hardest cases. At a red light, a customized Harley pulled up beside me. Its beefy rider lifted his visor with a tattooed hand and spit on the ground between us. "Rice burner," he muttered, the standard insult Harley-holics direct at the better-engineered, lighter, and cheaper two-wheelers from Japan. I smiled back, and cranked the throttle at the green. He led for a second, as his big V-twin's torque hit, and then the magic power bump of my Yamaha arrived, and I pulled ahead, lifting my butt in the air. It was a cheap, meaningless, macho victory. Of course, it felt great.

I found my way onto the idyllic Queen's campus, a medley of limestone, red brick, granite, and ivy.

Prof. Friedrich inhabited a book-stuffed space in the back corner of the Humanities building. I had to wait for a hangdog male student to leave before it was my turn. A heavyset, graying man in his mid-fifties, the Prof. regarded me dispassionately over half-moon glasses while I introduced myself and explained that I was researching the JFK assassination. He inspected the motorcycle helmet in my hand.

"Are you perhaps sent by my jokester friends in Anthropology to test me on some new crackpot conspiracy?" he asked, with a tinge of a German accent.

I said no, and explained that I had no theory myself, but just wanted to verify some facts, an approach which he seemed to approve of. Or should I say, of which he seemed to approve? I'm reasonably well read – for example, I consumed all of Virginia Woolf's books for a reading course in university. But something about heavy-duty academics makes me nervous.

"Let me begin with this: Who hated Jack Kennedy enough to want him dead?"

"Not the public, certainly," he said. "As is well known, he brought energy, youth and glamour to the White House. Most Americans, even Republicans, recognized his charisma."

"What about those who were not so public?"

"Then," he answered, "as they say in the delicatessens here, pick a number."

I started to correct him – magicians say "Pick a number;" deli staff say "Take a number." However, I recalled from my own spotty postsecondary career that academics do not relish being corrected.

He held up a finger. "First of all, the Bay of Pigs invasion, when Kennedy refused to provide air support or reinforcements, turned Cuban exiles and the CIA against him. Kennedy repeatedly ignored or went against Agency advice. He also angered the American Mafia, who had hopes of regaining the fortune they had invested in casinos in Cuba or hidden in cash there. Let us not forget that the CIA actually enlisted Mafia leaders like John Roselli, Sam Giacana, and Santo Trafficante to coordinate spying in Cuba and even plan Castro's assassination, so the organizations already had a working relationship. Plus, the Mafia were out put – I mean, put out – by Attorney General Robert's crackdown on organized crime."

He held up another finger. I was beginning to see a pattern. "Second, Hoover, and therefore all senior FBI factotums who had their noses between his buttocks, hated Jack and his brother Bobby, both for their womanizing and for stealing the spotlight from the Bureau's own crime fighting when the Kennedys took on the Mafia and its corruption of organized labour, especially the Teamsters."

"So," I said, slipping it in quickly before a third finger went up, "I guess big labour hated JFK too?"

"At least Jimmy Hoffa, and the Teamsters, and their allies," he agreed.

A fourth finger went up. He could count. "Then, there was the military high command. They despised Kennedy's handling of the Bay of Pigs, but there was one more thing they hated him more for – the Cuban Missile Crisis."

"I thought the brass would be happy that he made Krushchev back down," I ventured.

"Perhaps, but few in the public knew then what JFK had pledged in return – removal of American nuclear weapons on Turkish soil, whose presence made the Russians very nervous indeed. Those missiles could have incinerated Moscow before the Russians got anything close to the U.S. The generals felt that Kennedy had given up a significant strategic advantage for little in return.

"There were many in the military and intelligence spheres, too, who worried about Kennedy's stability and trustworthiness. He and his brother Bobby kept their own counsel and made their own decisions. This both enraged and frightened military and intelligence leaders, used to leaders like Eisenhower who listened to all their advice and then chose the best compromise.

"The Kennedys were unpredictable, unruly outsider cannons on the deck of the ship of state. In fact, Johnson is supposed to have told his mistress around the time of the assassination, 'Those bastards will never embarrass me again.' It was well known that JFK's own conquests included women who also slept with mob chieftains, journalists, foreigners, wives of CIA spies... who knows what pillow talk he was trading to satisfy his sex addiction? He also suffered from back pain, Addison's disease and other complaints. That meant he was on many medications, including strong analgesics."

The professor spread his hands wide. "Is this the kind of person you'd trust with state secrets, or control of the world's largest nuclear arsenal?"

"What *about* LBJ?" I asked.

"Oh, Johnson almost certainly hated Jack Kennedy," he continued. "They vied for the Democratic Presidential nomination and Johnson could not abide losing. He was endlessly ambitious, and yet older than JFK. Conceivably, had JFK lived, he would have been re-elected; and by then Johnson's moment to grasp the golden ring would have gone for good. Also, there were consistent rumours that Johnson himself might come under investigation for illegal activities around the time of the assassination."

"JFK's death was very convenient for LBJ, then... he got the Presidency and quashed the investigations somehow," I said.

"Exactly," Prof. Friedrich said. "As to whether he was involved, or knew of it ahead of time..." he shrugged. "Of course, also, fringe and extremist groups such as the John Birch Society and Ku Klux Klan hated Kennedy because they felt he was too liberal on civil rights, and too soft on Communism."

"What you're telling me, then, is that just about every organized, powerful group in the USA at the time wanted Kennedy dead?"

"Except perhaps for Irish Catholics," he said. My God – the man had actually made a joke. I think.

"My last question, and then I'll ask no more of your time. What about Oswald? What could have been his motives?"

"Oswald is a complex question. He is a figure in a house of mirrors. Which is the real Oswald, and which just a reflection or distortion? He certainly seems to have been a Communist sympathizer, learning Russian and having lived in the USSR. But why then, at the height of the Cold War, was he allowed to return to a normal life in the USA? By the time he started passing out those Fair Play for Cuba pamphlets, almost certainly he was a double or triple agent, a provocateur set loose to test the waters of pro- and anti-Castro sentiment. It has been established that he attempted to assassinate retired General Edwin Walker, a John Birch member and Texas gubernatorial candidate, with a rifle shot through ta window of the General's home.

"Perhaps he did shoot JFK because he disapproved of Kennedy's embargo of Cuba and Castro's losing his Russian nukes. Or, Oswald may have participated in the assassination purely for money; he had trouble getting and holding any well-paying job, but did have some military skills. There is one other possibility. Some sources suggest that his true target was Texas Governor Connally, who himself was seriously wounded on Nov. 22, 1963. Of course, Oswald was shot by Jack Ruby before he told investigators anything very useful."

"You mean, in that last scenario, he shot Kennedy by *accident?*" I said in surprise.

"It's possible. And it's possible that someone else shot Kennedy at the same time, on purpose. The whole affair, and the investigations and inquiries following it, are a Pandora's box for historians," he concluded. "So much evidence, so many measurements and kinds of documentation... and so few hard, fast, absolutely indisputable facts. How many gunmen? How many shots? Did the fatal bullet strike from the back or front? Was the bullet found on Governor Connally's hospital stretcher actually one that had struck him? Was the Governor hit by the same or other bullets as Kennedy? Why did the Secret Service rush JFK's body out of Dallas police custody so quickly? Why did the FBI do the same thing with Oswald's rifle? There is one sure fact, and that is that someone hated Kennedy enough to gun him down in cold blood and full daylight, beside his elegant wife."

"Or several someones," I said. I got up, thanking him.

"There is nothing new you wish to tell me, now that you have asked your questions?" he said, eyeing me curiously. This guy had intuition as well as brains.

"Not right now," I said. "But if I find any hard facts, I'll let you know."

He nodded and spun in his chair to stare out at the rapidly darkening sky. A bank of sombre clouds was lit from behind by a sun the hue of a Bloody Mary. Rays punctured the clouds like sniper shots. I was suddenly thirsty as well as hungry.

Chapter Eight

As I rode off in search of a restaurant, my brain was whirring. Friedrich had not mentioned anti-Catholic sentiments as a cause, but Gavin was by his very nature a loner, eccentric. He was his own movement. Others representing the forces Friedrich had named could have recognized Gavin's worth as an outsider, a Canadian to boot. With no obvious connection to their cause, they could have chosen him for precisely that reason.

Even if that were the case, who would care enough now to murder Owen and try to steal any evidence he might have? Was some multi-generational cabal still keeping a lid on the facts? It was stretching even my imagination.

In today's world, poets are natural believers in conspiracies. After all, they are born with a subtle talent which society does not value, while barely literate rappers and hip-hoppers make millions spewing their insults and boasts in crudely-worded chants. It's a mad, mad, mad world. Must be a conspiracy, since poets are "the unacknowledged legislators of the world," according to one Percy Bysshe Shelley... an objective observer if ever there was one.

After a forgettable but filling meal, I bundled up and prepared for a cold hour back to the County. Despite the arctic chill in the air, the night was exquisite. On straight stretches of the road, when I wasn't surrounded by cages (cars, to non-bikers) and 18-wheeled behemoths trucking furniture and pizza dough here and there, I could tilt my head back. Then I'd catch the constellations sparking like a diamond display set in dark velvet. A slender moon arced over the horizon.

Just as I turned onto Highway 49, my engine idling, I felt as much as heard a distant ringing.

What was it? I remembered that I had shoved my cell phone into my jacket pocket. I parked on the side, got my helmet off, and finally answered the damn thing.

It was my favourite cop. "You're not going to believe this," she said breathlessly, after we'd done the usual "Where are you?" dance. "I printed those shells, and we got a hit from Interpol."

"Whose prints were they?" I asked.

"Lucien Sarti. Looks like he really did handle those shells, just as old Owen wrote."

"I thought he was dead. Weren't his his prints deleted long ago?"

"Maybe someone in authority wasn't convinced Sarti was killed in Mexico. There seems to be some doubt about that."

"Did you say Interpol? As in the International Police Organization?"

"That's right," she replied. "Listen to what its fingerprint submission site says: "Interpol maintains a database of fingerprint files from member countries; currently, this database contains 47,000 fingerprint forms. The information comes from all member countries and contains very interesting data which can be made available to other member countries respecting the Interpol rules on cooperation." He never committed a crime in Canada to my knowledge, but seems to have been active in a few other countries."

"Very interesting is right," I said. "That's the first hard proof that Gavin wasn't just blowing smoke rings at us."

I told her what I had learned from Friedrich. "Of course, it's way out of my jurisdiction," she said. "But what a list of suspects! Sounds like you could interrogate just about anyone in the States alive then with a gun and a cause."

"Or a big bankroll," I said. "Any news on the suspect from the car crash?"

"Nothing directly," she said. "But someone did hotwire a car and drive it away from a used car dealer's in Picton last night. It turned up in Belleville today with traces of blood on the steering wheel and seat covers."

"So you've got DNA... but probably nobody to match it to."

"That's right," she said.

There was a pause, during which I could hear faint background voices, as if we were sharing someone else's conversation.

Then she spoke: "Are you heading back to Owen's place?"

"Yes," I said. "Should be there in about 20 minutes... why?"

"Is it OK if I meet you there?"

"Is this official or friendly?" I asked.

"Let's just say it's related to an ongoing investigation," she replied.

When I navigated my way back to the house, she was waiting outside in a small SUV. I invited her in, took off my helmet, jacket and gloves, and offered her a glass of County wine. She took off her own coat, revealing a dark green blouse and knee-length black skirt. She had a nice shape, I noticed, my observation no longer impeded by holsters, notebooks and tactical batons. Her dark brown hair appeared softer than when piled under a cop hat.

She accepted the glass and sipped it, looking a bit nervous, a quality I hadn't observed in the self-confident police officer I'd met – what, two days ago?

"What's the nature of your investigation?" I inquired.

She looked me in the eyes and said one word: "You."

"Is this when I ask for my one phone call?" I teased.

"No, this is where you answer a few simple questions," she replied, putting down her glass. "Such as: Are you attached? Are you straight? Do you like me?"

A little nonplussed by her directness, I killed time by pulling a Prof. Friedrich on her. I held up my hand, and enumerated digits. "One: no, or not exactly. I have a friend in Toronto, but we're not exclusive with each other. Two: as an arrow. Three: yes. Now do I get a turn?"

"Seems fair," she said, smiling for the first time. "What are your questions?"

"Just one. Why me?"

I looked into her jade eyes, and saw a tear forming at the edge of one. "I felt something between us as soon as we met. You probably don't have much idea what it's like working in a small place like this, where there are few female police officers."

"No," I said, and opened my arms. She walked into them, and rubbed her forehead along my chin. We hugged; she felt firm and soft at once.

"It's not so bad being a woman on the force any more. We have rights, and most of the male officers admit that we do as good a job as they can – sometimes better. But I feel I'm in a fishbowl. People here know me, although they still consider me from away. I can't date any County guys for fear I'll have to arrest them for drunk driving. If I hang out with a local man, everyone at the detachment is asking me about it the next day. Also, it goes unsaid, but I think it's still true ... a man who has lovers is called a stud, but a woman who does the same is a slut."

"You don't strike me as slut material," I said.

"I haven't struck you at all yet," she murmured. "Maybe later. But you might help me develop some slut skills."

With that, she hit the light switch, leaving the living room illuminated only by a night-light and faint moonlight through the windows.

"So you chose me because I'm an outsider and not one likely to tell tales about you?"

"There's that," she said, unbuttoning her blouse to reveal a white lace bra that shone dimly but fully. "Plus, you're a poet. Doesn't every woman want to inspire at least one ode?"

"I'm flattered," I said. "But I wasn't expecting... I didn't bring any..."

She pushed one hand gently over my mouth, and with the other flipped a foil-wrapped square in the air. "To serve and protect..." she whispered.

She unsnapped and shrugged off her bra, and then grabbed my belt, leading me over to the couch. "Let's not talk right now, OK?"

I nodded and kissed her, hard. She pushed me down and knelt over me, her brown nipples erect in the moonlight. Good taste, or more accurately the lack of fresh metaphors for a process which everyone knows, prevents me from detailing the rest of our evening together. Let's just say she was tender, passionate, very appreciative (it turned out she'd been celibate for more than a year), and no handcuffs or other police paraphernalia were employed. Yet.

Yes, I liked her.

At some point, we'd interrupted our getting acquainted long enough to go upstairs to the four-poster bed and throw on clean sheets, which didn't stay clean for long,

The next morning, I woke alone. The sun through a window threw golden trapezoids on the wall above my head. Downstairs, I found a note on the kitchen table that read "Thanks for everything. You're not bad – for a poet. I went back to my place early. Arrest you later... Mar"

I made some coffee in the automatic percolator, and thought about what to do next. Richard had told me he wanted Owen's killer or killers found. I was sure that one prime suspect was now chilling wherever County criminal cadavers were stored for autopsies. The other guy had no doubt beat a strategic retreat by now; Belleville had bus and train connections to the rest of Ontario... or he could have rented a car. I didn't even know if his first name was Hank, or if that was his partner's.

My primary brief was still to protect the Owen family from undue attention related to the long-ago activities of their black sheep. It was intriguing that the burglars appeared equally interested in suppressing the evidence. Interested enough to shoot Gavin and make it look like a hunting accident....

Wait a minute, I thought, *where would two out-of-County guys with a hunting rifle and a need for privacy stay? Not one of the well-known inns or hotels, where a credit card could leave a trace.* There were, I realized as I flipped through the local yellow pages, many B & B's here, but staying in someone's home and sharing their breakfast sounded like more intimacy than professional hard guys would want.

If I were them, I'd go for one of the hunting/fishing camps or cottages I'd spotted on my rides through the area. You stayed in a separate cabin, made your own meals, kept to your own schedule. All the proprietors would expect was payment up front; no doubt cash was acceptable. As long as one reined in one's behaviour enough not to frighten the walleyes lurking offshore, you'd be left alone.

I thought up a plausible story and started calling. In a big city I would have gotten nowhere with hotel staff on a flimsy pretext like this, but people out here didn't mind chatting.

I struck out at the first three places. The fourth was a place that rented cottages to the rod-and-gun set on the Long Reach of the Bay of Quinte.

"Bide-a-wee Cabins. Good morning to you," answered a woman's voice.

"Sorry to trouble you with this, ma'am," I started. "I met these two fellers at a bar last night, Hank and his buddy whose name I forget. Anyway, they were real friendly and invited me to visit them today and maybe do a little hunting together, but I wrote down where they were staying on a matchbook…"

"And now you can't find it? It's a good thing it wasn't my name you wrote down," she giggled.

"Anyway, ma'am, they said they'd been there about a week – do you have a couple of gentlemen like that renting one of your cabins? They'd be staying without their wives, and probably no kids or dogs either."

"I just might," she said.

"I know you want to protect your guests' privacy and all, but is there any way you could leave them a message to call me? Just say if I got the right guys, it's Jim they met at the Moose's Antlers last night? And if not, never mind and sorry to bother them?"

She agreed, and then said, "Hang on; their cabin's not far from mine. I'll just take a little walk over and see if they're in. Then you don't have to wait for them to call you back."

"That's real nice of you," I said. "I didn't catch your name."

"Verna," she answered brightly. "Now don't hang up."

I waited and tapped my fingers on the table. Lately, I'd got interested in drumming – with hand drums, not a big, noisy kit – and was working on a difficult rhythm where one hand played in threes, the other in fours, and every so often the shifting beats would meet exactly, then gradually go out of phase. I don't think I'd ever got it right, but even the mistakes were worthwhile. My metrical musings were interrupted by Verna, who sounded less perky and more troubled.

"Well, they're not there right now..." she said slowly. "Their car's gone. But their door was open, so I called and then went in."

"Yes?" I encouraged.

"Well, this is odd. It looks like one of them has left for good... one closet is empty, and there's only one shaving kit left there."

"Maybe they had a drunken fight after they went home," I said. "Anyway, it doesn't sound like a good day for hunting with them."

I thanked her and hung up. I called the OPP detachment; Mar was out on patrol somewhere, but another officer took down Bide-A-Wee's location and promised to have someone check it out.

I felt at a loss for what to do next. Now that I'd passed on the lead and the OPP had, or was getting, evidence from the safe deposit box and the two shells... what should I follow up? I could poke around Owen's house some more, but I had the feeling that, based on his pattern so far, he wouldn't have hidden anything important there. Or would he double bluff posterity, and do what others would assume he wouldn't?

I could do what poets are supposed to be good at: let thoughts and associations flow freely, and see what stuck. This sounded like as much of a plan as I was going to develop, so I decided not to put off visiting Sandbanks Park and its dunes and beaches any longer. After all, I'd look like an idiot returning to the Big Smoke and admitting to my friends that I'd passed on the chance to experience the "the largest baymouth sandbar separating freshwater in the world."

I packed the half-full bottle of Baco Noir in my saddle-bags, along with a fresh notepad and a good fine-line marker. If I got nabbed for illegal transportation of an opened bottle of alcohol, at least I could plead that a) I hadn't drunk any today b) I personally knew one of the County's finest, who might intercede me for me, and/or c) I was just a clueless visitor from the big city who didn't know any better. The last was probably the only one that'd get me off the hook, and not subject Mar to another round of in-detachment teasing.

I found a set of back roads that avoided any settlement of more than a few houses and eventually led me along East Lake Road. I stopped at the park entrance booth, willing to pay for a day pass like a good citizen, but no-one was home. The road curved along beside the lake and then I was at West Lake Beach. I found some reasonably firm ground in the sandy parking lot, parked my bike, collected the wine and sketchpad, and walked between some tall, bush-covered dunes. Wow. The beach was a long crescent that stretched as far as I could see to the north and west. At my left it ended at some low sandstone cliffs – the site of a once-popular inn called the Lakeshore Lodge, according to the map.

The beach was pretty clean, too, with a rim of crunchy zebra mussel shells a meter or so from the water's current edge. Good-sized blue breakers were sailing in, cresting in creamy lines and then crashing onto the sandbars. Sandpipers and gulls patrolled the littoral (*always wanted to use that word*). I walked a good long while, and then sat at a picnic table and thought nothing. The interplay of water, wind and sunlight was enough to occupy me for several minutes. I had a few swallows of Baco Noir, and toasted myself, the only human on the vast beach.

Lines started to form in my mind. I wrote them down. Yes, for those not moved to write creatively, it is a bit like taking dictation. You don't know where it's going to go, or exactly who is feeding you lines, but you have to trust the process. Sitting down and planning to write X usually produces unsatisfactory results, unless you're composing for the greeting card market.

> "Rewind from the President's exploding skull
> to the first hit, and then unlose
> innocent moments where smiles snap
> like flags in a stiff wind, and all the agents
> and officers are just doing usual escort duty,
> history is soft, yet to be set,
> and the world-version that was not to be

can live again... but the God of clocks
calls in a big negatory
on that one, and time
continues to expend its best in the
worst
way possible...."

Was this a poem, let alone a good one? No way to tell yet. But nothing else came, so I watched the waves some more, took my boots off and indulged in a barefoot walk along the damp sand. Two more good slugs finished the Baco Noir.

I considered penning a note that read "Help! The Prime Minister of Canada is keeping me as a secret sex slave in his County cottage and forcing me to read Hansard to him," corking it in the bottle, and tossing it in the lake, but didn't. Was I sober enough to ride a bike that could do 0-100 km/hr. in under five seconds? I found a long smooth log partly embedded in the sand, and made a deal with myself. If I could walk, boots on, from one end to the other without slipping or losing my balance, I was good to go. So I did, and I was. But I did ride carefully, not tigering the corners, and leaving lots of room when around other traffic. To adapt a saying popular among pilots, there are old riders and bold riders. But there are few old, bold riders.

Back at the house, I tried Owen's computer, but the thugs had effectively wiped his hard-drive and all its programs. I spent an hour an hour sorting through paper on the table, but found nothing likely to trouble his heirs, other than the fact that his unborn novel *Wry Aged* was not going to be a best-seller.

My cell-phone rang. It was Mar.

"Hey, Shakespeare," she said. "Got some news for you."

"What's that?" I asked. "You can't live without me?"

"Not exactly," she said. "Good work on tracking the perps down to Bide-a-wee, by the way."

"You're welcome," I responded. "Now give... what did you find out?"

"We found a 30-06 bullet under the bed. No rifle though."

"Any prints?"

"Just some partials," she said. "Someone had done a pretty

thorough job with a towel dipped in diluted bleach... but we did get a hit on the stiff."

"Who is he?" I asked.

"A Yank... Donald Perez, last known address in San Diego. He has one assault on record, and before that was in the US Marines for a while."

"Just like Oswald," I said. "Any clues as to who hired him?"

"Not so far. What are you up to next?"

"Actually," I said, not having had a plan until she asked, "I think I'll go back to Toronto for a few days. The trails I was following have ended or run cold. Plus, I need to replenish my wardrobe."

"OK, but don't stay away too long," she said. "If I have to drive two-and-a-half hours for a booty call, you're paying for the gas."

"You've got a deal."

We spent a few minutes reminding ourselves why we liked each other.

Chapter Nine

When your survival is threatened, your whole life is supposed to flash through your mind. In my case, though, the moment was more existential. Camus once wrote that when you stand at the edge of a cliff, your fear – that shakiness in your legs and gut – comes from the urge to throw yourself over. When death offers you the exit door, do you care enough to fight? Accepting the easy way out at least keeps you from worrying over questions like this anymore.

I had checked the county map and realized there was another way to find the 401 and Toronto. I could turn off the Loyalist Parkway at Carrying Place – what a great name that was – and cross the Murray Canal, then head through Brighton and join the four-laner going west. This looked like a decent alternative to the previous route along Wooler Road. So I packed my gear in the saddle bags, donned helmet, leather jacket and boots, and got going. I turned right at a substantial old red house that looked like a former inn, and followed a long easy curve with the lake shining to the left. Glancing into my mirror, I saw a big, dusty looking dark blue pickup truck trailing me. It had the usual he-man appurtenances, extra spotlights on the roof and a grille protector that reminded me of the "roo bars" Aussies mount in the outback. It was jacked up on its suspension, a mini-monster truck with tinted windows that kept me from seeing its occupants.

The truck wasn't crowding me exactly, but neither was it staying far enough back. I accelerated a little to increase the gap. It matched my speed. Ahead was a thinly populated stretch with bush on both sides. There were some substantial trees along the side. Feeling as much as hearing the rumble, I looked back and saw the truck pulling out to pass. I moved to the right of my lane to give the oversized beast room. I realized with a shock that it had slowed to match my speed rather than completing the pass. I still couldn't see anyone inside clearly. Instinct told me to hit the brakes. I did, throwing me forward in my seat just as the truck swerved into my lane. The truck's rear bumper grazed my front wheel, just enough to throw my bike into a weave. I struggled to control it, swerving off onto the soft gravel shoulder.

A big oak to the right stood ready to add my name to its tally. This is when Camus' question came back in the quantum-slowed moment that an accident occupies: Do you know why you are living? If not, then the logical alternative is suicide. Take the leap. I had no kids. I had accomplished some things as a poet, but never as much as I had hoped. I had loved some women, shared time with good friends. If my life ended now, it wouldn't be a tragedy.

But I wanted to know why somebody – more precisely, a whole group of somebodies, with pickup trucks, hunting rifles and God knows what else – cared enough about my inquiries to do me in. Why had I left my usual pursuits of writing poetry and investigating bookstore thefts and stolen manuscripts, for the unpredictable perils of this massive, tangled conspiracy? In this weirdly elastic second, the oak loomed up at me. The truck slowed, its driver waiting to see if I'd survive. I did.

I kept my hands loose on the handlebars, got on the pavement, executed a quick 180, and went back the way I'd come. I kept on the throttle until the truck was out of sight, pulled in behind a converted church and waited to see if the truck reappeared. It didn't, so I carried on along to Wooler Road and the 401.

I had gotten used to the relaxed pace and empty roads of the County in October. Toronto was a shock to my nervous system – so many cars, people, buildings, agendas – and I'd only been away a few days. How would it seem after a year in the County?

I called Sarah, who was soon to leave for a librarians' convention in Syracuse. I did my laundry and checked the messages on my office answering machine. It's cheaper than voice mail. You pay once for an answering machine that lasts five or ten years. You pay every month for voice mail.

Most calls were the usual junk; overdue library books (not from Sarah), phone solicitations for wonderful three-day stays in resorts avoiding any mention of hidden costs, moving guys with heavy Moldavian accents. Fyodor, if I ever do move my pitiful possessions, you'll be my first choice.

But two calls caught my interest. One was from a well-known author, a middle-aged woman named Fiona Teasdale whom I had never met. She'd won acclaim for her poetry and then started to write poetic fiction. Her first prose effort, *Spinning Into*, received largely ecstatic reviews. The second was from an unidentified, younger woman who said tersely: "I hear you're snooping into Gavin Owen's business. I got something to tell you about him. Call me."

Fiona Teasdale was a potential client. Her message had mentioned my assisting her in an unusual matter, and the freelancer's balance sheet is such that it's never wise to turn down work. You can go months without even the rumour of a suspicion of a job. I'd heard that she was, for a literary writer, reasonably well off – something about inheriting a few small apartment buildings in Toronto. I called her first.

After we'd exchanged literary pleasantries about each other's work (I was secretly pleased she'd actually read mine), Fiona got down to business. "I'll tell you why I called. It's about a major literary grant."

"You want to give me one?" I guessed.

"Sorry, no. It's about one I didn't get," she said.

This was a new one for me. There are always more writers than grants and prizes, and winners seem to be chosen by processes that invoke chicken entrails and loaded dice as much as literary merit. In a small literary scene like Canada's, it was all too possible that the writer you rejected for an anthology, or your ex-spouse, would be on the jury considering your next grant request or contest entry. Everyone knows this, so it's rare that anyone hires a PI to figure out why. You just shrug, buy an extra lottery ticket, and try again the next time.

"How can I help you?" I asked

"You can set my mind at ease," she replied. "If I was

turned down for the grant purely because the other applicants were doing work at the same or a higher level, fair enough. Maybe it'll be my turn next time. But, in all fairness, inasmuch as one can be fair when one's own writing is the issue..." She took a deep breath.

"Maybe you should just tell me what happened," I prompted.

"All right," she agreed. "I really thought I was in line for one of the advanced grants. It would have bought me a year just to work on my next novel. I could have paid a manager to look after my properties. Two of the people on the jury had written very complimentary reviews of my last novel. Of three advanced grants awarded, two went to people I feel are as deserving as I. But the third and last one went to a young man going by the name of Bar Zero. I'd never heard of him before, but supposedly he's a prodigy who has blazed his ways through zines, graphic novels and inter-active virtual world narratives – whatever those are – and now is writing his first literary novel. I haven't seen any of his writing, but just by reputation he seems an odd choice for a senior writer's grant."

"OK. What do you want me to do?" I asked.

"I'll pay you for a couple of days' work. Just find out what you can about him and his writing. If he's good enough to deserve the grant, fine. But if there's something fishy going on, I want the world to know." I agreed. I had almost worked off the advance Richard had given me, anyway, once I totted up my trav-eling time, expenses and hours on the job. She gave me the list of the jury members, and I promised to get back to her soon.

Doing Ms. Teasdale's little job would put me in little peril of being shot at. I hoped.

Actually, it was not only bullet-free, but took only a day.

I couldn't find much about the personal life of Bar Zero from the oblique, often joking biographical notes in the works I found on-line or bought from alternative bookstores. But one of his graphic novels had a note in the last frame – "Want more? Contact shivermetimbers@..." followed by his handle on a well-known and fast rising social networking site. I joined, searched for his profile name, and hit pay dirt.

The young idiot had posted for the delectation of his friends a photo sequence called "Cougar Hunt." In a mock erotic tone, with visuals reminiscent of Italian fumetti comics, he described seeking and finding a hot older babe to show him what men and women could do for each other. Although he gave her the name Caressa Lotz, I recognized her from another context: she was Veronica Jorgenson, a famously loudmouthed playwright whose fame had outpaced her talent. She also happened to be on the jury that had turned my client down in order to award the third advanced grant to Bar Zero.

But online photos can be faked.

I trailed Mr. Zero as he finished his shift at an alternative music store. He wasted an hour in a coffee bar, doing the wireless thing with his laptop, probably sending himself adoring blog comments under various pseudonyms. Then he checked his phone and seemed to recall an appointment. He rode his nicely retro Schwinn Flyer bike slowly enough that I could follow on foot to a veggie restaurant called Parsley Dressed.

There, I was rewarded by the sight of Ms. Jorgenson locking lips (and probably molars) with the young talent. I sidled to a table at the other end of the narrow eatery, ordered a drink, slipped out my digital camera, zoomed in and waited for the next embrace. It didn't take long. They were trading tongues again before their baked goat cheese endive drizzled in raspberry comfit had even cooled off. I got a few nice portraits of trans-aged lust with their waiter in the background, and then paid for my celery juice smoothie. I slipped their puzzled server a twenty to sign a note verifying that he had served the couple in the photograph on the date in question.

I went back to my office, printed out the pictures, added the note, and sent an email to my client telling her I had proof that the process had been rigged. I also, wanting to keep some shred of integrity, confessed that it had only taken me a day. I wish all my cases were that simple.

It was time to close up. I had a date with Sarah, and the evening was wearing on.

I was surprised to hear a knock on my door. Surely, it couldn't be another client. Two in one day? My system would never recover from the shock.

I opened the door, and a skinny twenty-something woman with hair dyed various colours of red and green, a lip piercing and a couple of Celtic knot tattoos on her visible anatomy, walked in.

"You Aaron Miles?" she asked.

"Yes... in fact you're looking at the entire staff of the Aaron Miles Investigative Agency," I confirmed.

"What?" she said. I could see that hopes of building a witty, rapid-fire Spencer-style repartee were slim.

"Have a seat. What can I do for you?" I asked.

She sat. "I'm Cassie de Groot. You been nosing around old Gavin Owen's place in the County," she said. I wasn't expecting that.

"I can't confirm what I do for other clients. There's a reason I'm a private investigator" I replied.

"What if I hired you?" she asked.

"Well, if I were already nosing around old Gavin's place, as you put it, that would be a conflict of interest," I said. She frowned, puzzled, mouthing "conflict of interest." I was getting the sense that, as they say on gardening shows, she was not the sharpest tool in the shed.

"Can you explain what you want me to do, exactly?" I tried again. "That would tell me whether I can work for you or not."

"I want my baby to get what's owed to him," she said. This was beginning to feel like one of those surreal conversations in which each statement has no connection to the previous one. Perhaps someone would turn into a rhinoceros next.

She pulled out a snapshot of a chubby-cheeked boy with dark red hair, maybe eight years old. "I've tried to talk to the Owens. They wouldn't give me the fucking time of day without some proof."

I was about to ask the obvious question when she pulled an official-looking form out of her fake crocodile bag and slapped it on the desk between us. It had a few strands of grayish hair stapled to it in a small plastic bag. The letterhead read DNAtivity Lab Report. It duly verified that DNA testing indicated that the owner of the hair was in fact the father of Vincent de Groot.

Well, at least she wouldn't be suing me for paternity. My hair wasn't that gray yet. Maybe just tastefully frosted here and there.

"That's right!" she said triumphantly. "Gavin Owen is the father of my child, and that makes Vinnie his only, whaddya call it…"

"Heir? The hair makes the heir?" I ventured.

"That's right. And I don't trust those rich bastards no further than I could throw them," she said. "I want you to find out what that my son has a right to."

"Didn't Gavin own a house?" I asked.

"Yes, and that's worth something," she said. "But I heard" – She laid a finger beside her prominent nose for emphasis, "that he had some big secret which could be worth a lot – maybe turn into a book, a movie, who knows? I want you to find out what it is. A little bird told me you already know a shitload about Gavin Owen and what he was getting up to."

"I'm sorry, I can't take this job," I said. "But I do wish you and your son well. You should be able to get the Owens' attention, now that you have DNA evidence. If you don't mind my asking, how did you and Gavin get together?"

"Oh, he and my grand-dad were in the same Orange Lodge. Gavin met me when I was about 19 and looking for work. He suggested I come and clean his place once a week for cash. I did that, but it was obvious the old goat wanted more than his floors done. I thought, why not? Wasn't like I was a virgin or anything, and I needed the money. So I'd do him a couple of times a month and he'd pay me.

"The last time, before I came to Toronto, the condom musta leaked or something. I didn't know for sure he was the father, 'cause I had a BF then too."

I looked blank.

"Boyfriend, dummy," she said, rolling her eyes. "Anyway, the BF said the baby didn't look like him, so he split. I raised little Vinnie all on my own, figuring I'd hit old Owen up for money someday.

"Then I read in the paper that he got dead. I got one of my friends to bust in his house right away and get me a sample of his

D-whatever so I could get it tested."

That must have been the first break-in that Mrs. Eagle Eyes had reported, the one before I got there.

"You know breaking into someone else's house is illegal?" I asked.

"Who cares? I didn't do it," she said, popping her gum. I figured the concepts of conspiracy and abetting were beyond her, so I didn't bother.

"So you can't help me?" she asked.

"No, I really can't. Sorry," I said.

"Screw it, then. You want a quick BJ?" she said. "I got a half-an-hour to kill."

I thanked her graciously. She actually replied, "No problem." I said I was on the way to see my girlfriend. She left and I locked up.

What is it with kids today? She hadn't offered a movie, dinner, or even a reason. Where's the romance?

Chapter Ten

I talked again to Richard. What else did he want me to do on the case? He advised me to sit on it for a little while. No news (at least to the public) was good news as far as his family was concerned, and maybe the OPP would snag the killer before he got out of the province. But he asked that I stay in touch, as there would be work to do closing down his uncle's house. He would be happy to pay me for it. I thanked him, stunned at my good luck. There must be a long work-famine period coming, because for a freelancer, I was feasting .

I got another message, this time from a formal-sounding lady at Markham's, one of the biggest international art auction houses. Mrs. Wanger desired a meeting to discuss a possible assignment for me. Fine, I was ready for a change from all this conspiracy stuff. A nice simple art job – a purloined illuminated manuscript, perhaps – was just the thing I needed to lift my spirits. After the arts grant job, I'd be batting two for two.

At 2:30 the next day, a secretary ushered me into her office. Mrs. Wanger was tall and slender, with short brown hair and bifocals, a crisp grey suit and ruffled white blouse. She rose from behind her steel and glass desk to shake my hand. After the greetings, I commented on the fact that the only art on her office walls was a large framed picture of her with a dashing-looking man and two Mini-me boys.

"I work with art all the time," she replied. "With the constant parade of colour and form, it's restful to look at white walls once in a while." She offered me coffee, which I accepted. I figured that the stainless steel high tech system sitting on her shelf would turn out a better cup than my battered aluminum percolator. It did.

I ventured the "How can I help you?" gambit. Examining my card, she asked, "What exactly does a Cultural Systems Investigator do?"

"Pretty much anything legal that's related to art, literature, music… and that requires discretion," I answered.

"Art," she said. "Our auctions command record prices for artists because of our reputation for integrity, which includes a careful provenance for everything we list for sale."

"Provenance as in who owns it, where they got it from, and so on all the way back to the artist's studio?" I asked.

"Precisely," she said. She extracted a framed print from its cardboard case and slid it onto her desk. "What do you know about this print?"

It was a beauty. "This is one of the red, black and blue versions of probably the most famous Inuit stone-cut print ever created, Kenojuak Ashevak's The Enchanted Owl," I said. The owl, with its eyes suggesting a shamanic presence within and feathers arching into an aura, was as crisp as the day the print was pulled over half a century ago. "According to legend, the artist and print-maker couldn't decide whether the image looked better in black, blue and green, or black, blue, and red, so 25 were printed of each colour combination. It was one of the most popular Cape Dorset prints right from its release. But when the Post Office put it on a stamp to commemorate the Northwest Territories' centennial, its value went through the roof."

She was silent, eyeing me in an assessing way. I couldn't tell if I had impressed her yet, with my knowledge gleaned from a couple of summers working in an Inuit art gallery, or had just tried too hard, so I upped my trivia a notch. I mentioned that Inuit prints had to be one of the few positive things to come from cigarette packages. A southern or "kabloona" (thick eyebrows in Inuktiuk) artist, visiting Cape Dorset in the early 50's, offered a cigarette to an Inuit friend. Examining the Players package, the Inuit commented that it must take a long time for an artist to hand-paint the tiny sailor's head, the word "Hero," and all the other details on each package. Realizing that his buddy had not yet been introduced to the concept of multiple prints from an original, the Southern artist explained the process.

"We could do that," the Inuit man is supposed to have replied, and annual sets of prints started to appear from northern art cooperatives a few years later. An artist would do a drawing, the design would be cut into a soft soapstone plate; technicians would ink it, pull the copies, and then destroy the plate once the edition quota was filled.

Finally, she responded with a hint of a smile. "I'm glad you know something about Inuit art. And The Enchanted Owl's price has continued to climb," she added, "it hit $58,000 at an auction in 2002... unfortunately, not one of ours."

"Look at the details at the bottom," she directed. I did, noticing the stylized igloo "chop" that signified the Cape Dorset co-op, and the pencil-written notations giving title, artist, and edition number. "It's the 21st print."

"Right," she said. Typing rapidly on her large laptop, she pulled up the website of one of Canada's most respected art galleries. She clicked her mouse a few times, and then turned the computer so that I could see the screen. It was another copy of the same print. Then she zoomed in on the details, and I read "21/50."

"Wait a minute," I objected, "there can't be two prints numbered 21, unless someone goofed in the numbering, and therefore there are actually fifty-one or more, copies out there."

"This is our problem," she said. "As you know, the value of limited edition-prints is maintained by being able to assure collectors that there are only fifty, or however many, made. There will never be more to dilute the exclusivity of their copy."

"So where did this one come from?" I asked.

"It's offered on behalf of the estate of a Canadian doctor, Arnold Martin, who moved to the Dominican Republic a long time ago," she said. "His daughter Valerie is his heir, and she's selling some of the estate. I want you to go down there and find out whatever you can about its provenance. Where did he get it from? We need to know whether this copy, the gallery's, or both, are fakes. Obviously we can't auction the print until this question is answered."

"The Dominican... instead of staying here for a whole

Ontario winter?" I joked. "That's a tough choice."

"We will of course pay your airfare and all expenses," she said. "We also will arrange for a Spanish-speaking driver to help get you around and translate as needed."

Before realizing I was trying to talk my way out of an instant vacation, I blurted out "Won't sending me there cut into your profit from the auction?" She smiled: "Yes, but our reputation is worth more than that, and if we ever get another Enchanted Owl to auction, I want to make sure the edition number is going to be valid."

I found a contract in my briefcase, and she signed. She also filled out a retainer cheque to cover my initial expenses – airfare, hotel deposits, and the like. Although I wouldn't want to work full time for one of these large organizations, I do appreciate their financial resources – when I get a piece of them. Mrs. Wanger gave me a neatly typed list giving contact information for my guide/translator; Valerie Martin, the daughter; and a local representative of Markham's.

After a four-and-a-half hour flight on which the seats seemed to be narrower than ever (it couldn't be that I'm getting wider), I landed in Puerto Plata. The sudden heat was a revelation; I could feel my bones sucking it up as if they were straws. The airport was under construction. We shuffled down corridors with blank concrete walls and translucent plastic sheeting waving in the wind. A local band of middle-aged guys standing in a corner struck up a sprightly melody, putting some energy into it despite the heat and humidity. I slipped them a U.S. five and got big smiles in return.

Outside was a cacophony of guys shouting and waving signs: limo, hotel shuttle or tour drivers, taxi drivers. I caught a hand lettered sign reading "SR. MILES" out of the corner of my eye and focused on the young, goateed guy waving it. Identifying myself, I shook his hand and he introduced himself as Esteban. He led me past a nice display of palm trees – during Canadian autumns, it's easy to forget that things elsewhere in the world continue to grow – to a battered grey van.

Esteban was friendly, quite fluent in English. He said he'd learned it caddying on one of the island's golf courses and then informally renting cars to tourists. "Here in Dominica," he explained, "we're big on informal." He was tall and lean, with a rapper's oddly accented delivery. "Call me S," he smiled. He flipped up a cover between the seats and offered me a bottle of anejo (aged) rum, after taking a swig himself. "Welcome to de best rum in de world, mon," he laughed, achieving a kind of Dominican-Jamaican patois.

I figured *screw it, I'm on vacation, sort of* – it was caramel-smooth, with a nice kick. This was obviously the single-malt Scotch of rums. I was used to dark stuff with a heavy molasses flavour best concealed under a shot of Coke. He said it was about half an hour to the hotel, so I settled back to enjoy the sunlight and sugarcane fields we blasted by. S kept his window open, shouting comments and greetings to other drivers, pedestrians he knew, and girls too shapely to be passed in silence. They smiled at the attention rather than giving him a stare and middle-finger salute. I was beginning to like this place.

I couldn't believe the traffic. The variety of conveyances fascinated me – trucks, taxis, large and small cars, burros, vans, and hordes of tiny single-cylinder motorbikes, some carrying two or three adults and children, nobody with a helmet or leather jacket. We stopped at a red light, and I was startled to see all the bikes, and not a few cars, pass us on either side and run the light. "In the DR, traffic laws are, how do you say, an optional," Esteban said, noting my surprise. "I obey most so I don't freak you gringos out." "Appreciate it," I replied.

I was struck by the fertility of the land, dry as it looked. Tall fields of sugar cane grew everywhere, and tropical flowers thrived along the roadside. There seemed to be a national election campaign in progress – large posters of various candidates, mostly Hispanic-looking (the average Dominican self-describes as "mixed," with skin colour running from whiter than mine to dark chocolate). I noted that the locals expressed their disdain for certain candidates by perforating their signs with gunshots. One sleazy-looking guy had the wind blowing through his forehead.

My hotel was in Sosua, a beachside town a half-hour drive from the much bigger Puerto Plata. "Daytime, this is good family place," Esteban said. "Bring the kids, lie on the beach." "And at night?" I asked. "Sin City," he laughed. "The professional ladies are out on a couple of blocks, and men tourists come to buy." "It's legal here?" I asked. "Only the pimp get hassled," Esteban said. "The ladies got a business like anyone else, *no problemo.*"

This made a lot of sense, I thought. The world's oldest profession is never going to go away as long as men are men and Viagra is cheap. Take the pimps out of the equation and the prostitutes get treated better. Plus, they keep nearly all of what they make, so there's no economic need for extra hijinks involving "husbands" or "boyfriends" showing up with a gun and relieving Mr. Gringo of his whole wallet. "You like, I take you there tonight?" he offered. "Thanks, man, but I'm here for business," I replied. He shrugged.

We agreed to meet at nine the next morning. After a somewhat confusing phone conversation with Valerie Martin – a bad connection, and at first she thought I was a Spanish-speaking caller – she offered to discuss the print with me. She added "My place is sort of an island whenever water levels are high, so I'll meet your car on the dry side. I have a jeep that gets through most things."

The next morning – another fine, clear day – Esteban and I drove about ninety minutes. As we left the tourist areas and headed into the highlands, I was fascinated by the roadside scenes. It recalled to me that you don't really *get* another culture in the big cities. It's out in the villages and countryside that the true differences appear. I was intrigued by how many homes had some little business running with a roadside stand – a few bunches of bananas or plantains, green coconuts, fried lunch, questionable-looking meat cuts, even some colourful paintings and contorted carvings. And the banks – they seemed to favour buildings the size of a large phone booth with a teller/manager the only worker and barely room for a customer. We were frequently passed by local buses – noisy, oversized vans stuffed to the gills (and then some) with people, bags, and the odd goat or chicken – roaring along more on less on schedule, and the hell with the potholes.

Valerie proved to be a cheerful, full-figured woman in late middle age with dyed red hair, beads and bracelets, and a flock of children of various hues about whom she said "I've sort of adopted them." We all piled into her very ancient Land Rover, painted in a medley of red and grey primer, and which she started with a screwdriver stuck into the ignition key slot. I looked dubiously at the spate of dark-green water flowing between us and her hacienda. "Not to worry," she said. "Old Diablo has never failed me yet," she added, giving the dashboard an encouraging slap. A small bolt fell onto the floor mats, but she ignored it.

We plowed through the water in great style, sending up tsunamis while the children yelled. I noticed S had his eyes closed, offering up a silent prayer. We hit ground, though, and the Land Rover shuddered, dug in and hauled us up to the hacienda, where we immediately got a tour from Valerie. The place was a comfortable rambling affair, alternately finished in stucco and palm thatch with an atrium, hammocks here and there, and a few plants growing up through tiled floors. To say the late Dr. Martin was a collector would be high praise – he was more of a hoarder. We visited rooms full of antique weapons, dusty stringed instruments, local dolls, and rusting metal toys. His taste in art seemed indiscriminate, terrible landscapes sitting side-by-side with brilliant portraits and still lifes, no particular regard to artist, subject, or quality.

It was his book collection that took my breath away, including leather-bound tomes in Spanish that went back to the 1600's. "Probably the finest historical library on the island," Valerie said, "but I don't have the money to maintain it the way it deserves." I agreed, noting the foxing on the title page of a beautifully printed volume about the early history of the Caribbean. I ran my thumb over the Gothic text, feeling the indentations of letterpress printing.

"But you didn't come here to talk about books," she said. Esteban excused himself to go for a walk. We sat down at a battered dinner table, sipping excellent Presidente beer that one of the older kids served us.

I explained my mission, and showed her photos of the two 21/50 prints: the one she had sent for auction, and its ringer in a gallery collection. She checked each picture with a magnifying glass, sighed and was silent a minute, rubbing her face meditatively.

"This may seem irrelevant," she ventured, "but what are

your politics? How do you feel about the haves versus the have-nots? Do the poor deserve their status because they don't work hard enough?"

"I'm pretty much an old lefty," I answered. "As far as I'm concerned, rich people generally don't deserve their wealth. Either they inherited it or they stole it... just more legally than the guys who get caught heisting banks. There's a Navaho view of wealth I rather like. When they see someone showing off a big house, fancy cars, or a private plane, they ask "Who is he not helping?"

"Here, like in most Third World countries, and more and more the First World too, there is a big underclass of people with not much, and a small overclass of rich assholes who fix everything to suit their comfort and continued wealth," she said.

I nodded.

"OK," she nodded. "Let me show you something." She led me to a room with big sliding drawers locked by impressive padlocks, selected a key from her crowded ring, and opened a drawer. She lifted out a stone-cut printing plate and laid it on the floor. It sure looked like the plate from which "The Enchanted Owl" was pulled. I ran a finger over the carefully-incised reverse image, and a trace of red ink came off.

I looked at her, raised an eyebrow. "It's the real thing," she said. "My dad once worked at a hospital in Montreal. Innu with TB used to get flown down there for treatment. He cured one guy who sold him this plate for a few hundred bucks. He used to work pulling prints for the Dorset co-op, and instead of destroying this one, he kept it for a rainy day."

"So, your number 21 was pulled from this plate?" I guessed.

"Right," she said, "with the help of a local artist whose name I won't mention. The whole scam was my idea; no reason bit players should suffer the consequences."

"And have you made other copies?" She nodded. "There's a #47, and a 12 out there that nobody's spotted yet. They sold well."

"And what did you do with the income?" I asked. "I'm guessing you haven't blown it on a new SUV or home repairs."

She looked me straight in the eye. "No. Or cosmetic surgery", she added, flipping her double chin with a finger. "You've only seen some of the kids I support. There's actually fourteen of them, living here most of the time. Some were just one too many kids for the family income. Or, the parents moved away and pretty much forgot about them. Maybe the father wasn't the husband. I also fund a girls' school and orphanage in a nearby village. It was built by a missionary and philanthropist, but he died and his family didn't want to keep paying for the upkeep and groceries."

"I'm impressed," I said. "I think this is the first time Robin Hood has taken up art fraud."

"I'm telling you the truth here. I got into this fully knowing it was wrong, and probably illegal too, although I doubt the DR has many laws about art fraud. If I go to jail for it, so be it... but I'd do it all over again. Tell me, do you think a rich, pissed-off art collector or museum somewhere in North American, Europe or Japan matters more than a bunch of kids who are getting a second chance to thrive?"

I nodded my understanding of her position, and stood up, "I'm going to walk around your island, and think about what to do. I'll have an answer for you in half an hour." I went outside and did just that. At first, I was followed by a flock or giggling kids, but they tired of trying their few English words on me – "Chew-angom? Comeek book?" and went back to the house. I put my moral question to the lizards and the gulls. I dipped my hands into the fast-flowing river and thought. Esteban was dozing in the shade of a palm tree. I woke him and he willingly verified the existence of the orphanage and school and their positive influence on the lives of local children, offering to do a drive-by on the way back to the hotel. I told him to join us in a few minutes and went back to the house.

I was thinking of my old, sadly late, friend Henry. At first a promising director of experimental documentaries, he had diluted his talent with a taste for vodka and idleness. But he was still a great talker up to his last year, and loved nothing more than discussing "situational ethics." He even subscribed to a little rag called *The Situationalist* to feed his habit. "There is no absolute right or wrong," Henry would pronounce. "Laws may say so, but it depends on who's involved, what's at stake, the needs of those affected... Even the justice system, for example, can't say it's always wrong to kill. Police can kill when they or someone else is threatened, citizens can do so in self-defence. What's wrong one day is right the next." Henry would have been proud of my reasoning now.

I also recalled the old Watergate conspirator, G. Gordon Liddy, said on his speaking tour with Timothy Leary that some actions could be legal but immoral, and others illegal but moral. Of course, were he here now, he'd probably shoot me first and ask questions later. Valerie was outside, showing some of the children what to pick from a vegetable garden. She straightened up, rinsing the dirt from her hands with a watering can.

"Well, Mr. Cultural Investigator, whatchoo gonna do?" she asked.

"I appreciate what you're doing for these kids, and I think your heart is in the right space. As far as the auction house's print goes, though, the jig is up. You email them in a couple of days, with a copy to me. Tell them I helped you find a letter in your father's papers that proves the print is bogus. Apologize for unwittingly sending them a fake, but don't mention exactly where it was printed. You and I will take the plate and destroy it now."

She nodded, not too displeased. "And what about the other Enchanted Owl prints I, um, helped with that are out there?"

"Their owners didn't hire me, so I'm going to classify those prints as not my problem. As I understand the art auction business, none of the auction income goes back to the artist or the co-op, right? So it's not like the Inuit are getting ripped off by your prints. It's people who were a little lazy about checking provenance."

"They should have hired you," she returned, giving me a little elbow dig.

"No, I just got lucky... someone at the auction house figured out that there were two copies of the same print number floating around. All I did was follow clues."

"We have a deal," she said and gave me a muscular handshake. "I'll go get the plate now."

"Wait," I said, struck by an impulse. "Who's the most downtrodden kid you have here?"

"Natalia. Her parents would beat her for the least little thing. She's afraid of her own shadow. "

"Send one of the big kids to find her and a hammer," I said. Guessing my intention, she did just that, and went into the house.

Valerie reappeared with the plate at the same time an older boy returned, dragging a smaller girl behind him by one hand. She was slender, big eyes surveying the world behind a tangle of dark curls. I took the hammer from the boy, pointed to the plate which Valerie had set on the ground, and offered the hammer while Valerie explained the task to her.

At first, Natalia shook her head, trying to hide behind the boy who had brought her. But he gently pushed her forward, and finally she shyly accepted the hammer. Its haft looked thicker than her forearm. She shot a questioning look at Valerie, who nodded and made a swinging gesture. Natalia grabbed the hammer with both hands, swung it over her head, and broke the plate into five irregular pieces with a resounding thud. She smiled for the first time. The other kids cheered and clapped. I picked up the pieces, selected five eager apprentices to throw a piece into the river, and said to Esteban, "We're done here."

Valerie encompassed me in a maternal hug, and we hydroplaned back across the river in her four-wheel-drive chariot. Back in the van, Esteban and I did stop at the school and orphanage, where I saw nothing to make me regret my choice. The place was clean and cheerful, and the girls in their blue uniforms looked healthy and adequately nourished, proud of their art and writing adorning the walls.

Ensconced in my hotel room, I decided to extend my situational ethics to a little scam of my own. I'd be saving the auction house not only their reputation, but also any lawsuits that could result from their selling the print. They could afford a couple more days of my investigative work in the Dominican. So I phoned their local representative, explained that I would have an answer soon and things were going well, and thoroughly enjoyed a few days of lounging on the beaches at Sosua and Cabarete, where kiteboarders sail over the afternoon waves like skipping stones. I continued to investigate the *anejo* rum, and realized that I'd found a new friend.

I did cast a few thoughts over my inquiries back in Canada, but came up with nothing definitive. I'd have to be back in the middle of it to figure out what was going on.

Chapter Eleven

Back in Toronto, I had a nice, relaxing evening with Sarah. She was pleased with the rough amber piece I'd bought her from a mine in the DR. Fortunately, I'd remembered my promise and also picked up some champagne and a tasteful bouquet with a flamboyant bird of paradise in the middle. I told her about the wonders of the Dominican Republic, and a bit about what I was paid to do down there. She didn't ask about my love life in the County, and I didn't tell... yet.

Our arrangement was worked out after consulting articles and a book about polyamory relationship, and a lot of negotiation. Casual flings didn't have to be shared, unless the other asked directly. Occasionally we did share them, both to build trust and for the voyeuristic spice it added to our own conjoining. Anything that seemed to be moving toward serious emotional involvement did require revelation and discussion, though, because that could shift the underpinnings of our comfortable and sporadic relationship.

The next morning, Sarah left for her convention. For want of anything better to do, I went back to my office. I could always catch up on my least favourite part of running a sole practice: paperwork, both that which various government agencies seemed to generate solely to keep themselves in business and the mail. Letters for years had been exclusively a formal affair; gone were the days when *billets doux* from besotted lovers or catch-up notes from long-lost friends arrived in handwriting with a stamp on them. Today's harvest included an appeal for me to be listed in the North American Library of Private Investigators, a prestigious sounding tome that was really vanity publishing. People unsure of their own worth paid to be honoured. I passed up on the $89.95 fee to receive the authentic plastic wall plaque certifying my importance.

My phone rang. "Is that P.I. Studly?" a woman's voice asked. It took me a moment to place it.

"I guess; is that Mar?" I returned.

"Yes, it is. Listen, I've got some disturbing news for you."

"I don't get a choice between good or bad news first?" I asked.

"The good news is you get to talk to me again. The bad news is the evidence is missing... the shells and Owen's manuscript."

"Missing? From where?" I asked, dazed.

"Our evidence locker at the detachment," she said. "After we got the warrant for the manuscript and did that initial fingerprint check of the shells, we were going to send it all off to our regional Forensic Identity and Photographic Services. It's gone."

"Who had access to it?" I asked.

"Anyone who works at the detachment, I guess. You're supposed to sign out the key and log whatever you add or remove. There are guns, seized drugs, contraband tobacco and alcohol, and all kinds of stuff from investigations in there. But whoever took the Owen evidence somehow forgot to log it out."

"So what happens next?"

"There'll be an internal investigation... maybe by the Special Investigations Unit."

"It's got to be a cop or civilian who works there, don't you think?" I asked. The thought crossed my mind that the morally flexible Ms. de Groot, who had already told me of contacts in the County willing to bend or break the law on her behalf, might have engineered this. But I hadn't told her anything about the shells or the memoir. Plus, she hadn't struck me as the kind of criminal genius who could organize a theft from a police detachment.

"Likely," Mar answered. "We're interviewing everyone who was on shift during the last twenty-four hours."

I contemplated telling her about my meeting with de Groot, and the revelations about Owen's previously unacknowledged son. Cassie wasn't my client, so confidentiality didn't apply. On the other hand, there was no link that I could see between her and the hit men. I suppose she had a slender motive to get old Owen knocked off so her son would inherit, but according to her she wasn't even sure he was the father until after Owen's death. I decided to hold that card for later and we hung up without many sweet nothings. Oh well, she was probably at work, anyway – not the venue for double entendres.

The person I did owe was Richard. I phoned him and explained what had happened. When I mentioned the missing evidence, he was alarmed.

"You mean it's out there and nobody knows who has it at present?"

"Nobody but the perpetrators," I said. "The OPP has an investigative unit looking into it but that could take a little while."

Richard was silent for a few beats.

"I want you to go back there," he said. "If the evidence turns up, we need someone there representing the family interests."

"You mean helping keep it out of the news," I said.

"That's a big part of it. The other thing is, we're going to list his property for sale. It would be useful to have someone there to keep an eye on the place and meet the real estate agent. I can get people in to clean and fluff the place before buyers start arriving, but I can't take time off from work. How about you give us one more week and I'll pay you another $2500?"

I would be lying if I said I thought twice about his proposition. The Owens were turning into my primary employers. My bank account could climb back into positive numbers for the first time in a while.

I updated the message on my answering machine, closed up the office, and went through the routine of changing clothes, packing a few necessities, and getting ready to hit the road for the County. I picked up a newspaper while I was replenishing my shaving kit at the drugstore, and a small article caught my attention, titled: "Owen Investments Mulling Merger with Fremont Financial." The article, which avoided the tedious alliteration plaguing its headline, said that Owen Investments' net worth approximated $150 million, and its solid management and client base made it attractive to the larger Fremont outfit. Fremont had offered to keep current staff and executives in place should the merger take place.

Hmm. With $150 million at stake, give or take, I could see why Richard was so concerned about his family's current image. Having a relative involved in the most controversial assassination of the past century was not going to raise the family firm's market value.

My journey east was a rewind of the last one, except that it was a cloudy day and the cold was getting into my bones. Not that many riding days left, I reflected. Winter is a melancholy time for bikers and gardeners in Canada; both groups spend time dreaming about what they'll do in the spring. I skipped the Palace of Fried Meat.

On one of the county roads, to commemorate the coming end of decent riding weather, I picked a stretch where I could see a mile or so in either direction. There was no traffic, so I wound the throttle, only easing off when I briefly saw 200 kph on the speedo. My eyes were watering from the cold air pushed under the face shield. The motor still had a few revs left to go, but there is this Draconian law in Ontario: if you're nailed going more than 50 klicks over the limit, police confiscate your vehicle and your license for a week, plus hit you with a huge fine. That was an experience I could do without, so I coasted back to a relatively sedate 100. It took a while for my smile to subside.

Nobody appeared to have kept up the break-in tradition at the house. I let Mar know I was back, then phoned the real estate agent, Mrs. Knudsen. She was a nice older lady who eventually dropped by to borrow the house key and make a copy. I had also phoned various contractors on the Owens' behalf. Few of them seemed to return calls, so I asked Mrs. Knudsen about this.

"Oh, you'll have a time of it, all right," she said. "So many people with money have been moving up here that anyone who's a plumber, electrician, builder or renovator is probably making more than the local lawyers. They've got work coming out of their ears. Unless they already know who you are, or they're related to you, they won't even call back. That's the way it is." She promised to ease the way for me by calling a couple of the more reliable contractors, who owed her a favour.

I was enjoying a solitary dinner of the last of the local peaches-and-cream corn and a nice filet of pickerel when I heard a vehicle pull up beside the house. I went to the window and saw Mar get out of her SUV.

I opened the door and she gave me a warm hug. "Welcome back, "she said. "Any new conspiracies to report?"

I updated her on Gavin's purported son, and his mother's interest in Owen's possessions. We sat together on the back step and watched the sun sink into the mostly bare trees. They looked like many-fingered black hands reaching up to snag a red ball. I was starting to think like a poet again.

We held each other for a while there as the air chilled. It was comfortable, as if we had known each other far longer. We went inside and made love silently, and that was gentle and tender. I may not own much, but sometimes I feel like the luckiest man in the world. A beating heart and functioning lungs, a new poem on the way, a loving woman, October skies; what else do you really need?

She left early before I was fully awake. But she hadn't been gone that long when she called me again.

"Guess what?" She said. I was too drowsy to play, but she didn't wait. "Constable Turley's gone AWOL."

"Who's Turley?" I asked.

"One of our detachment's not-so-finest," she said. "We nicknamed him 'Turkey.' In a year here, he's gone through an angry divorce, wrecking a cruiser in a single-vehicle accident, an assault-on-a-suspect allegation, and losing his house to the ex. When he didn't show up for his shift, we did some checking. He cleaned out his room in a boarding house, and his bank account, and no-one's seen him for a least a day."

"Sounds like suspicious behaviour," I replied. "What's next?"

"We've put out an APB for him. He drives this old muscle car, so unless he's changed vehicles, someone will spot him."

Chapter Twelve

She was right. As I heard on a local radio station, ex-constable Turley got as far as Napanee, about 30 km east of the County, before an alert officer spotted his 396 Chevelle and pulled him over. Mar told me later Turley had over fifteen thousand in cash on him, but no shells or manuscript. He refused to say anything about the missing items or who had put him up to the theft. Maybe they'd paid a lot more than a few thousand dollars.

I updated Richard. He suggested I make Turley an offer: his family would pay Turley's legal representation, up to $20,000, if he'd tell me who had the missing evidence.

I waited for the cleaner Richard had contracted and then left the house in her hardworking hands while I rode into Belleville. Turley had been transferred to the regional jail while he awaited arraignment.

He was led into the interview room in cuffs. Turley was a large, puffy-looking guy with heavy five o'clock shadow on pale skin and small, suspicious eyes. I don't think the orange jumpsuit was the best colour for his complexion.

I introduced myself and laid out the deal. Before I'd finished talking, he was shaking his head.

"No way," he said. "Do you have any idea who these guys are?"

"I have some idea," I said. "For a start, they're from the States. Secondly, they don't place a high premium on human life."

"You got it," he said. "Anyway, I can afford a lawyer now. Even if they convict me…" I gave him an eyebrow at that, as it seemed a pretty open-and-shut case to me. "I'd rather spend a couple of years in the slammer than forever in a coffin."

I plied him with a few of the persuasive tricks I'd learned in a university course on rhetoric, but nothing was working. Fear is the strongest convincer, and I could see from the sweat on his brow that somebody else scared him more than I could.

I spent a while back at the house fielding and making calls. It was dinner time, and I was thinking evil thoughts about a nice bachelor dish – tuna, egg noodles, and mushroom-soup sauce *aux pois verts....* when I heard a car pull up outside and stop. It was a BMW sedan.

Man, I bet this place had racked up more visitors in the last few weeks than old Owen had in a year. I opened the front door, and greeted a man in designer glasses and a nice suit, as he fetched a briefcase from the rear seat. Maybe another real estate agent, but he looked too slick for that.

"Brian Moriarty," he introduced himself with a light-but-manly handshake. "I have a business proposition to make to you." I explained that I wasn't the owner of the house, more like a temporary caretaker, but he cut me short with a wave of his hand.

"It's not about the house," he said. He turned, and I followed his gaze to catch the flash of reflected light in a pair of binoculars up the road. It was good to see my vigilant neighbour keeping her end up.

"May we talk inside?" I appreciate a man who can handle modal verbs, so I invited him in. He regarded the couch with some doubt, brushed off a cushion, and sat down gingerly.

"I'll assume that since you're here, you're working for the Owen family," he began.

I figured that, while my detecting duties came with a guarantee of silence, house sitting didn't. "Just looking after the place for them until it's ready to be put on the market," I said lightly.

He afforded me a flash of expensive white teeth, a smile that indicated more confirmation of his guess than actual amusement.

"I'd guess you're more than a house sitter," he said. "In fact, my practice also has clients who value confidentiality. They are willing to pay handsomely." He handed me his card, which identified him as an upstate New York lawyer.

"Let me guess. They want to publish my selected poems, but they want to keep their names out of it?"

He gave me a repeat of the not-amused smile. "Let's not waste each other's time. I have grounds to believe that there is certain information, and perhaps a few articles connected with it, that your clients wish kept secret. Oddly enough, that is exactly what my clients wish, too. You could get paid twice for doing the same job – with a clear conscience."

With a mildly theatrical flourish, he unsnapped the brass catches of the briefcase. Inside, a row of neatly bundled $100 US bills suggested he was carrying around several thousand dollars.

"This is yours, if you agree to two things: first, not to pursue the location of these items any further; and second, to tell no-one other than your clients what you've learned." he said.

"One question," I said. "Would these items possibly have been stolen from the evidence locker of a police detachment in this very county?"

He looked shocked. "My clients would never indulge in anything illegal."

"And if they did, they wouldn't tell you about it. Then you'd never have to prevaricate to others," I suggested.

His shrug was eloquent, a lawyer's finely balanced gesture that conveyed "Maybe yes, maybe no, but I'm not going on the record to say so." Hey, a justice couplet.

"I just have a teeny ethical problem," I said. "If, hypothetically, I were working for people who wanted to keep certain information and items quiet, I could hardly take the word of a representative of an unknown third party who had acquired these items that they would keep them secure. The items would belong to the original owner's family, anyway, as part of the estate."

It was a good thing I had experience in poetry. This whole conversation was becoming so indirect that I began to wonder if it was about anything real at all.

"Some people's ethics become more... flexible... when presented with ten thousand dollars," he said, running his hand over the bundles with a lover's touch.

"Maybe yours do," I said. He stiffened at the insult.

"Really, Mr. Miles," he remonstrated. "I've heard that you've been shot at and otherwise threatened. Can't you take a hint? Are your ethics worth more than your continued survival?"

"A good question. But you'd never threaten me, would you?" I asked. "That would be unbecoming for an officer of the court."

I got the smile a third time. "I'm not threatening you," he returned. "Just asking you to consider your own welfare as well as that of your clients."

"Can you get a signed and notarized undertaking that the items in question will be returned to any clients that I might have?"

"My clients are not prone to signing and notarizing anything," he said. "I'm afraid they prefer more direct action."

"Then take the ten thousand dollars back to them," I said, "Along with a message: I'm not the only one who knows what the evidence means. There's no need for further violence, but I will continue to do the job I've been paid for."

"You're certain? Then I'd suggest you keep the blinds down at night," he said, and closed and retrieved his briefcase.

He didn't offer his hand again, just drove off into the cool night. I felt a little shaky. He didn't scare me, obviously being hired as a mouthpiece rather than gun. What had scared me was my own desire for that money and the fact that I had to think for a second before turning it down.

The great Raymond Chandler once wrote: "However top-lofty and idealistic a man may be, he can always rationalize his right to earn money." I love that nautical-sounding word "top-lofty." But, ultimately, if your ideals are for sale, are they truly ideals? Or just options?

If you lose your own values, nothing matters. You're just another operative in a free-fire zone, and nobody much will care when you go down for the count. I must have been shaken, to be mixing metaphors myself.

What to do now? I sat on the couch and rested my head in my hands. But the room was too bright to think, so I shut off all the light and let my eyes slowly readjust. It's when things are dim that they can slip-shift into new forms.

OK, every avenue of inquiry seemed stalled for now, except one. How did someone get to Turley? You don't exactly phone or email someone you've never met and say, "Hey, how's it going? How about destroying your career and ripping off the evidence locker in return for a big heap of money?"

I phoned Mar and got her on a coffee break.

I explained my reasoning and asked, "Where did Turley hang out when he wasn't working?"

She told me about a seedy bar called Players Place that attracted the less savoury County residents. They didn't appear in glossy photos of wine tasting in free lifestyle magazines. Apparently Turley had become a regular there. Nobody would know me, which could be a plus or minus. At least they wouldn't make me for a cop right away.

I thought for a moment, then headed into Picton. I bought a tube of hair gel at the drug store and greased my hair up so it looked like oily porcupine quills. Then I picked up a stick-on skull tattoo and carefully applied it to my left hand. Perfecto.

I parked outside the bar and walked in, affecting a swagger. The regulars gave me a quick once-over, but nobody seemed very interested. The men looked gainfully unemployed, perhaps auditioning for a wanted poster if they ever got ambitious. The women looked like extras from a movie about a tragic country star's demise.

I sat at the bar, ordered a draft, and listened to what sounded like a heavy metal version of "Bad Moon Rising" on the bassy sound system. When the bartender wasn't busy, I motioned to him. I slid a folded ten over, which he covered with one hand as smoothly as topping off a pint.

"Seen Turley around lately?" I asked.

"Why you want to know?" the barkeep asked, not moving his hand. Until he pocketed the ten, he wouldn't owe me anything.

"Son of a bitch owes me a couple of hundred," I said. "He swore he'd pay me back by tonight. But I can't find him anywhere."

The barkeep laughed, and disappeared the ten. "Join the queue," he said. "Turley's gone straight from being a cop to waiting to become a con. He's in the joint in Belleville."

"Shit," I exclaimed. "You know anybody who can get a message to him?"

"You could try One Ball...big bald-headed guy with a handlebar moustache. He's usually in around now."

"Why's he called One Ball? Packing his jeans a little light?" I asked.

"Nah, it's because he's always leaving one ball on the pool table when he thinks he's going to run 'em and win. He chokes," he said, and walked off to serve a new customer.

Sure enough, a guy fitting One Ball's description stalked in a few minutes later, checked the talent out, and sat down at a back table. When he nodded to the barkeep's question "The usual?" I said, "Put it on my tab," and carried my draft and his Bud over.

"Thanks," he said, "but if you're looking for a cheap date, I ain't your type."

I told him my invented tale of woe about Turley and the two hundred bucks. He didn't look surprised. One Ball drained his Bud in a few gulps and said, "Thanks for the brew. No way I'm going to visit him in jail. He's bad news. But I ain't seen Turley in weeks."

He looked me in the eye, as experienced liars do. But, as poker players will confirm, nearly everyone has a tell. One Ball had started tapping his fingers on the table just as he told me he hadn't seen Turley in weeks. He was lying about that... maybe more.

I had no leverage on One Ball right now, but I had a feeling I could get some.

I thanked him and marched out of the bar. Outside I made a big show of starting up my bike, revving it noisily, and riding off. But I circled the block and parked it down a side street. I found a church with a shadowed doorway and stood there, engaging in the PI's major occupation: waiting for something to happen.

After half an hour, I was cold, bored, my feet were beginning to hurt, and I seriously needed to pee.

But I spotted my quarry leaving the bar with a young long-haired guy in tow. They stood beside an old Dodge truck in the parking lot and scoped the street, both men swivelling their heads around. They couldn't see me.

Then One Ball reached under his truck and pulled out a metal box that must have been held on with magnets. He slid the lid back and extracted a small bag of something, which he tossed to the young guy. His customer dabbed a finger in, took a quick taste, and handed over some bills.

I had him. One Ball went back into the bar. I figured this was his regular selling routine, and that he'd be out to service another client soon.

So I did what any right-thinking citizen would: I called the cops, asking for Mar. "How'd you like a nice little drug bust... a guy who might have a line on Turley's new employers?" I asked. I explained the situation, and Mar said she'd be over soon, with a partner.

They arrived about ten minutes later – no siren or lights. This time Mar had a patrol car with the police dog and his handler following in an SUV. They left their units next to my bike where they couldn't be seen from the parking lot and joined me in the church doorway, Mar making the introductions.

It didn't take long. One Ball came out again with a skinny woman in a black leather coat. Mar and her partner waited until Ms. Skinny forked over the money and then made their move.

Mar hit the pair with the beam from her big Maglite. The dog streaked over and stood growling, while the cops advanced with their hands on their guns. There was no resistance. One Ball obviously didn't like dogs, as he shrank from the furry officer, and in no time he and the skinny woman were seated in the rear of the cruiser.

Mar came over to me, while her partner called it in to the detachment.

"Thanks for the tip," she said. "How can I pay you back?"

"I can think of a number of ways," I smiled, "but what I most want right now is information. Sweat One-Ball – OK, maybe that isn't the best way to put it – lean on him. See if you can get him to roll on whoever paid Turley to steal the evidence. I'm betting he knows something about it."

"You got a deal, schlemiel," she said, and walked back to the cruiser. They took off for the detachment and I rode back to

Owen's house with the gratifying feeling of having won a hand in the poker game.

The next morning was grey, a fine drizzle falling. Colours seemed to be leaching out of the landscape in preparation for winter, when everything in Ontario goes grey, brown or white except for evergreens and the brave stems of sumacs. I didn't feel like getting soaked so I made a big pot of coffee and busied myself with getting the house in order. I sorted Owen's books, a curiously intimate connection with someone I'd never known alive. It was like a map of his mind, or at least his tastes. He was solid in fiction, poetry and *belles lettres* collections, questionable in politics and history, and off the scale in religious debate. How do you sort someone's library, anyway? I flipped open a translation of Caesar's memoirs, and there it was: "All Gaul is divided into three parts."

The wisdom of the past. So, three piles. Books to be pulped or donated to one of the local charity shops, books that could be sold in lots to a used-book dealer, and a much smaller pile of tomes with some value – old, rare, or first editions by known authors. To my surprise, I found pristine editions of early books by writers as disparate as Leonard Cohen, Charles Bukowski, and Margaret Laurence. He even had acquired somewhere an early Hemingway first edition inscribed to Morley Callaghan, who had once bested the bigger Yank in a famous amateur boxing match refereed by F. Scott Fitzgerald in Paris.

I amused myself for a moment imagining the ringside commentary for this brief exhibition of pugilistic prowess:

"Hemingway comes out of his corner, and he's leading with a short declarative sentence. But it's not developing the plot... and now Callaghan! Callaghan's coming in with jabs of detail – a left with an adjective! A right with an adverb! Hemingway's confused... he can't seem to find the core of his character! He covers his face... now Callaghan's working the body! A quick love scene out of nowhere! Biff! Kiss! Smack! Fitzgerald calls time-out; he wants to know when either competitor will develop the sense of doom so necessary to strivers in a soul-less civilization."

Fortunately, my cell phone rang, more entertainingly than

before. I'd figured out how to download a favourite Talking Heads song as the ringtone.

It was Mar again. "You were right about One Ball. He couldn't face another long stint in jail. So we got a name out of him in return for reducing the charge from with intent to traffic to simple possession. "

"Great," I said. "So who put him up to talking to Turley?"

"An old guy, lives out around Milford," she said. "We don't know much about him. He's never been in trouble here for anything. Name's William Harlan."

"Are you going to arrest or charge him?" I asked.

"So far we've got no evidence except One Ball's say-so. According to him, Harlan contacted him − One Ball is kind of the go-to guy for anything illicit around here. Harlan offered him $500 to set up a meeting with Turley; he says Harlan didn't want anyone seeing him and Turley together. Unless we find something definite to link One Ball and Harlan, we won't be doing much. I mean, if you were on a jury, who would you believe: a convicted druggie known as One Ball, whose real name, by the way, is Avery Milk..."

"I can see why he prefers 'One Ball'," I said.

"... or a nice old retired gentleman who pays his taxes and lives a respectable life, as far as we can tell?"

Mar added that Harlan's phone number was unlisted, but gave me his address and directions to a place just outside Milford on the road to Cherry Valley. We made a date for dinner at a gourmet restaurant in a village named Bloomfield. I wondered for a moment if the village had been named after the brilliant but short-lived Mike Bloomfield, a lead guitar prodigy with the Butterfield Blues Band back in the 60's. He had played on Dylan's *Blonde on Blonde* album, thus guaranteeing his immortality. Probably not.

Clouds still hung low and grey, but the drizzle had stopped. A plumber's truck arrived, and The Master of Pipes and his helper were now noisily engaged in disassembling the upstairs bathroom. Apparently, according to the real estate agent, the two rooms that most sell potential buyers are the bathroom and kitchen. Comforts of the body matter, obviously.

I was tired of sorting books and had made sufficient in-roads to feel justified in knocking off for a while. The roads were going to be wet, so I pulled my stunning orange rain pants over my jeans and rode at a cautious pace to Milford.

I could see where it got its name. There was a large pond, almost a mini-lake, whose outlet was through a narrow stream. It must have once powered a mill here. Every Ontario town of any size had an eco-friendly, renewable-energy-powered mill. *Where did we screw that one up?* I made a mental note to come back to this charming village, and found Harlan's place.

His house was medium-sized, white frame with blue trim. It was neatly kept; a bit sterile for my tastes. I noticed there were no bushes close to the walls, and the hedges were trimmed shorter than usual.

As I approached the door, I was surprised to note a little inspection eyehole, like one finds in city apartments, not in country places where many don't even lock their doors during the day. I activated the brass knocker and soon saw a blue eye, distorted, studying me through the spy-hole.

The door opened and I was confronted with a tall, rangy man who looked to be in his late 70s. He was balding, his remaining hair trimmed short. He wore a pinstriped blue shirt, neat black suspenders, and grey flannel pants. His blue eyes looked observant.

I handed him my card and explained that I'd been hired to look into the affairs and estate of Gavin Owen and some missing possessions of his that a Mr. One Ball might know something about.

"Young man, I have a few strict rules. One of them is that I will discuss almost nothing here except the sorry state of the Toronto Maple Leafs hockey team, the vagaries of the weather, and possibly the current wine crop. Only in a controlled environment of my own choice will I talk about anything else."

"Not even in your own home?" I asked, since he hadn't invited me in. This was clearly not your average easygoing retired County person. There was an icy firmness about him that suggested he was used to others following his wishes.

"If it amuses me, you may label me a paranoid old man. I

prefer the term "careful." We could have a nice chat in my living room. But perhaps you have associates secreted down the road ready to pick up everything we say with a parabolic mic or laser device that reads the vibrations on the window from our voices. Perhaps you have a wireless transmitter in your motorcycle helmet," he said.

"But you're OK to talk to me if you choose the scene?" I asked.

"Yes. Let's say out of perhaps misguided feelings of humanity, I am willing to tell you a story, strictly off the record. It might be instrumental in preserving something you care about."

"And that would be...?" I returned.

"Your life," he said simply.

I didn't see that I had much of a choice here. This was the only lead I had to work, and I had no sense that the old guy was threatening me himself, simply stating the facts as he understood them.

"What are your conditions?" I asked.

Rather than answering right away, he motioned me into his living room, and flicked on his TV, choosing the weather channel. After perusing the forecast for the Quinte region, he made a quick phone call, in a low voice. I heard a few terms like "ceiling", "tow" and "wind direction," and then he hung up, apparently ready to decide.

"Here are my conditions. Do you know the Picton airport?"

"Yes, if you mean the old military training one on the mountain," I said.

"The skies should be clearing. Meet me outside the Flying Club there in precisely two hours. Take it or leave it," he said flatly.

"Take," I said, nodded, and left.

I grabbed a pizza slice and Coke in Picton and spent an hour riffling through newspapers in the Library. I didn't learn much, except that teenaged girls who peak as stars around sixteen have troubled lives later on. Then, fascinated. I found that a Vancouver man named Jack was making waves by asking the Kennedy family for DNA samples to prove that he was JFK's illegitimate son, conceived with a Texas woman shortly after the 1960 election.

Chapter Thirteen

In my on-and-off career as an investigator, I've interviewed people in some unusual circumstances. But this one topped them all.

I wound my bike out in its lower gears, climbing the twisty route to the airport. Harlan was right... grey clouds were moving east, and the sun was out. The airport was a genuine WW II relic, with rows of decaying, dull-painted cedar-shingled barracks and a wooden watchtower. Various small businesses occupied some outbuildings and hangars, including an oddly sited boat operation. I found an open gate and rode in, following signs to the Flying Club. There stood Harlan, no vehicle near him. I guessed that he wanted to keep his transportation secret, too. A small Cessna took off in the background, its motor droning urgently.

He waited while I doffed my helmet and fastened it to my bike, then he laid a stern hand on my shoulder. Saying little, he propelled me to one of the disused barracks, looked around and then jiggled the padlock for a moment and led me in.

It was spooky in there – dusty and tinged with the smell of mildew. Rays of sunlight streamed through holes in the walls and roof, illuminating ruined beds and sagging tables.

A one-piece flight suit was hung over a chair, with a pair of running shoes below. On the chair reposed a lightweight flying helmet with a built-in mike and earphone, and a jack to receive a cable.

"Strip, and put those on," Harlan said.

"Strip? As in take my clothes off while you watch?" I asked, surprised.

Harlan snapped, "Young man, the deal was we do this on my conditions or not at all. I have been a number of things in my life, but homosexual is not one. I am not interested in your body. I want to make sure you're not hiding any recording devices now, or going to transfer anything while my back is turned."

"OK," I said. "But no cavity search."

For the first time, his mouth curved in a hint of smile. "No cavity search," he agreed.

Shrugging, I followed his orders. The flight suit fit reasonably well, and was warmer than I expected. No doubt some miracle fibre helped insulate it. My feet swam in the over-large shoes. Harlan observed this, and assured me that I wouldn't be walking far anyway.

We went outside to the base of a long runway, patched and cracked.

A friendly middle-aged couple had rolled a beautiful red two-seater glider out of a hangar. The tow plane was in front, a long rope stretching back to the glider.

Harlan flipped up the glider's canopy and motioned me into the front seat. "Keep off the controls until I tell you otherwise," he ordered. He plugged a cable into my helmet.

I'd never been in a glider before, although I'd flown in small aircraft, including a float plane.

The lack of a motor seemed to simplify things considerably. The cockpit was bare, with a polished plywood floor and thin upholstery on the seat. In front of me were a stick and rudder pedals, and a few instruments: an altimeter, a compass, and something labeled a variometer with a plus and minus scale in "fpm". Feet per minute? I guessed this indicated vertical speed, an important consideration for gliders.

Harlan walked around the plane, checking everything, then climbed in behind me. I twisted my head round and watched him check the rudder and aileron functions.

The male half of the couple looked at Harlan, who gave him a thumbs-up, and then stretched the rope until there was some tension on it. I heard a mechanical click behind me. Obviously, Harlan had activated the release, because the rope went slack, coiling away from the glider's nose. He did a quick communications check, ensuring that we could hear each other, and then, with a flip of a switch, that he could talk to the tow pilot on radio.

I was fascinated by one small detail. A tuft of yellow yarn was taped to the canopy in front of me. This seemed rather artsy-craftsy for someone of Harlan's no-nonsense disposition.

The canopy was snugged in place, and the rope reattached. The tow plane crept forward until the line was taut. The couple each took a wing of the glider.

The tow plane started to roll, and the couple ran alongside, keeping our wing tips in the air while the glider balanced on its single wheel. Soon they let go, and although the wings wobbled slightly, nothing scraped.

To my surprise, the glider rose into the air before the tow plane. I realized this made sense – with its long wings and low weight, a glider would not need as much take-off speed as the heavier tow plane with its relatively stumpy wings.

Harlan did an impressive job of keeping the glider skim-ming the runway, just a few feet up. Obviously he didn't want to get far above the tow plane at this delicate moment, or something might go awry.

Finally, the tow plane laboured into the air and then the airport shrank below us. Harlan kept the glider a little higher than the tow plane, the tow rope taut. It was comforting to see that he knew what he was doing. Our airborne "tractor" made a few lazy circles, gaining altitude, until I felt the glider suddenly lift as if we'd caught an updraft coming up the side of the mountain. Har-lan warned the other pilot of his intentions, then released the tow rope. Suddenly we rose and cut to the right. The tow plane went down and left, waggling its wings in a brief salute.

Harlan's voice cracked over the intercom. "Give me a mi-nute to gain some altitude and then we'll talk,"

"OK," I replied.

It was noisier than I expected. The wind rushed and whis-tled; the structure of the plane creaked and flexed. It was cool in the unheated cockpit but not uncomfortable, and I found the patchwork view of fields and roads below fascinating. As we rose, I could see several lakes – the reaches of Lake Ontario that sur-rounded the county, and then Lake on the Mountain. In the wavering distance was the long shape of what must be Lake Consecon. The altimeter kept winding up, the variometer went between plus and minus as we encountered invisible columns of air flow, and the compass swung as we circled and soared.

Harlan's voice woke me from my reverie. "I'll tell you the story now. Don't interrupt. You can ask me questions once I'm done, but I won't guarantee to answer them. You've probably guessed by now that, if you tell anyone what I'm about to relate, I'll deny ever having said it. I'm just giving you a little glider lesson. Got that?"

I said I had.

"Now grasp the stick in front of you and push it gently forward." I did so, finding more resistance than I'd expected. The glider's nose dipped, and we gained speed.

"Now center the stick, and then hold it to the left. At the same time, push the left rudder pedal."

As I followed his instructions, there was little response. I applied more pressure and the plane banked to the left and started to turn. I held the turn until we'd gone 180 degrees around, then somewhat clumsily brought us back to level flight.

I decided I liked gliding. It was quieter than motorcycling, satisfying in a different way. Both experiences included the pleasure of banking, leaning far into turns as the world tilted below. But a bike is always ruled by the growling urgency of its engine. A glider is in stealth mode, like sailing: you read the whims of invisible currents of air and compromise between where you want to go and what the conditions will allow.

"Not too shabby for a biker," Harlan said. "Now I don't have to lie about giving you a lesson. Release the controls, and I'll talk."

"A long time ago, an idealistic young man from a Midwest state, whose name was not William Harlan, joined the CIA right out of university. The Agency was really starting to flex its muscles then. With a Cold War budget and the "need to know" rules limiting oversight of what we were up to, the world was our playground. We'd engineer the ouster of a left-wing dictator here, publicly disgrace a Commie-symp news outlet there. Indochina, behind the Iron Curtain, Africa, the Caribbean, South America –

our operatives and operations were everywhere.

"Cuba was the first crack in our omnipotence. It should have been a snap to overthrow a young hothead like Fidel, but we couldn't pull it off. We enlisted the help of mobsters with Cuban connections, but they failed too. The problem was that Castro, despite his totalitarian tendencies, was making life a lot better for the average citizen than under that bastard Batista. Unless Castro lost his popular support, we couldn't get to him.

"We had a chance with the Bay of Pigs, but Kennedy wouldn't push it all the way and we ended up looking like losers. We weren't used to it.

"One day, a senior man in the Agency pulled me in, swore me to silence, and explained that the best thing any red-blooded, God-fearing, hand-on-his-heart American could do right now was to get that freak Kennedy out of the White House before he lost American's edge in the nuclear arms standoff with Russia or leaked some State secret to one of the many floozies who took dick-tation, as my superior called it, from the King of Camelot.

"Get him out how?" I asked.

"He's going to have an accident – a very well organized one," I was told. At the time, I was young and mindlessly patriotic. I didn't really consider the implications of an intelligence agency plotting to eliminate its own more or less democratically elected president.

I never pulled a trigger or gave a direct order to anyone to shoot the President, but I was in on some of the planning and gave logistical support. First the hit was going to take place up north, then in Tampa. But neither location turned out, so we were green-lighted for Dallas.

"I can confirm the broad strokes of Owen's account. Nobody involved in that operation knew everyone else, at least not by their real name. We were organized into operational cells. I can't tell you from how high up the chain of command of the CIA and the government the order came. We were just doing our jobs – like Eichmann a couple of decades earlier.

"There were three shooters. Oswald didn't know about the rest of the shooters or the plot. He was told, and paid, to begin firing when the presidential Lincoln reached a certain point. He did his part better than anyone expected; no-one thought that he'd actually hit the President with that cheap mail-order Italian rifle, let alone Connally, too.

"Oswald was just supposed to be a distraction, and it worked. The people who recognized the sound of shots turned towards the Schoolbook Depository. That's when the second shooter fired and missed and the Corsican on the knoll scored the head shot.

"Oswald was told he'd be picked up near the Textbook Depository and driven to a safe house. But he wasn't. The fool panicked, predictably, drawing attention to himself, and you know the rest. He was the goat we staked out to keep the public tiger happy.

"We had some operatives disguised as ordinary citizens dispersed around Dealey Plaza whose job was to give contradictory evidence – muddy the waters. They did this brilliantly. No one since has ever been able to sort all the pieces into a meaningful picture that finds universal agreement.

"After that, I went on to a long career with the Agency. I got my pilot's license and worked on some of the biggest successes (which few heard about) and failures, like Iran-Contra, which everyone heard about. Like many others, I helped ride herd on witnesses and Kennedy conspiracy theorists who were getting too close to the truth, planting disinformation or otherwise inconveniencing them. A few had to be terminated with extreme prejudice. All for the good of the nation, of course. I also developed a lifelong allergy to being recorded, photographed, or otherwise known to the public. That's why I took you on this flight; up here, we are the only ones who know what's being said.

"Before you ask me why I'm telling you all this now, let me save you the trouble. I'm trying to give you some context to understand the forces arrayed against you if you take your inquiries any further.

"The Kennedy assassination is where my country started to go off the rails. Do you know who coined the term 'military-industrial complex' when he warned the American people against its growing power?"

"Umm," I temporized, feeling like I was back in Grade 11

history without my homework done, "Noam Chomsky?"

"Way off... it was somebody you would never guess: the old military pro himself, Dwight D. Eisenhower. In the last days of his presidency, before handing the reins over to JFK. Eisenhower had the long view; he understood the need for a nuclear deterrent and strong military forces, but he hadn't forgotten that freedom was the most basic value on which the U.S. was founded. When the power of individuals and democratically elected officials was lessened, so was America's moral authority to represent freedom. I remember his exact words: "In the councils of government, we must guard against the acquisition of unwarranted influence, whether sought or unsought, by the military industrial complex. The potential for the disastrous rise of misplaced power exists and will persist..."

"Bush, Cheney, Rumsfeld, the Homeland Security Act," I said. "Right," he responded.

My attention was diverted for a moment by a huge cumulus cloud, which towered over us, gradually spreading out. I could see its shape changing subtly as tendrils and bulges of cloud reformed and drifted off. It was about as far from a military-industrial complex as you could get.

"How right he was. Kennedy's assassination, although it made sense to many of us at the time, was a disastrous misstep. Kennedy was a dangerous President, but he should have been controlled or impeached constitutionally. His murder confirmed that the Commander in Chief was just the public face of power; the secret decision-makers were the one who really mattered, the shadow government, if you like, of foreign and domestic intelligence agencies, the Pentagon, and organized criminals. Corporations, especially the energy ones, weren't far from the center of influence either. What's good for big oil is good for America. If it isn't, too bad for America.

"As Americans have become more fearful of the rest of the world following our retreat from Vietnam and then 9/11, our liberties eroded under the pretence of protecting us from enemies. The very military-industrial interests Eisenhower warned us about have been running the country for decades; it doesn't really matter who's in the White House, Republican or Democrat, because he's not making the decisions that count. That's why I left the States after my retirement and settled here in the 90's."

His voice stopped, and I realized it was finally my turn. Our glider had been describing gentle circles, but now we seemed to be headed back towards the airport.

"If you disagree with the course America has taken, why not tell the truth? Why help keep a lid on it even now?" I asked. It was odd talking like this, when I couldn't see his face. I glanced at the tuft of fabric, which had been streaming straight back from its anchoring tape. Harlan did something with the controls, and the tuft slewed sideways for a moment. Aha! My keen detecting sense informed me that this was a simple way of gauging the direction in which air was flowing over the canopy.

"Two reasons. One, I took an oath to protect every secret of the Agency, and this is the biggest one, even if I regret my part in it now. I do not take oaths lightly.

"The second is that, even though I no longer live in the U.S. or work for the Agency – except for keeping a distant watch over Mr. Owen, whose alcoholism and tendency to drop hints concerned us – I still love my country.

"Had the public learned the truth a few decades ago, it might have made a difference. Those hidden figures who engineered and carried out the plot could have been brought to justice and the movement for reform of our political processes might have been unstoppable.

"But today, despite its power and wealth, the U.S. is a fragile structure. It is hated by many other countries and nearly a billion Muslims around the world. The debts incurred by the Iraq misadventure are huge, and continue to grow. We built our economy on cheap oil and two cars for every family. Now oil is expensive and half our cars are made by manufacturers other than GM, Ford and Chrysler. Russia is no longer a major foe, but China has three times our population, nuclear arms, a larger army, aggressive tendencies, and a rapidly expanding economy.

"Destabilizing the U.S. further by revealing the guilt of many of those who have run it – either from the White House or other, less obvious centers of power – would be fatal. Don't forget that Bush Senior worked for and eventually ran the CIA and was active in the Agency around 1963. He was as devoted a servant of big oil as Johnson, who made concessions to Texas oil interests, and Dubya.

"Later the elder Bush became President, just like Andropov and Putin in USSR or Russia, who leapfrogged from the KGB to the Kremlin.

"When you let the spooks run your country, you're really in trouble. There's no arm's length, no separation or balance of powers. Intelligence agencies are supposed to operate in darkness, doing things that the visible government must deny knowledge of, but the government must still make final policy decisions. It's ironic that the same thing happened to the Americans as to the Russians. Anyway, if we came clean now, the vultures would gather and the American Empire will crumble even faster."

This guy did not go in for short answers. In another life, he could have been a ruthless university lecturer, the kind that won't slow down and enjoys writing big fat red Fs on student assignments.

"You said you wanted to help save my life," I reminded him. "What do you suggest I do?"

"Do nothing," he responded. "Leave it alone. People who knew less than you do now have been sanctioned in the past. Most of the original conspirators and operatives are dead, of course; however, there are still powerful interests who don't want the truth set free and will apply their power to ensure you don't do so. Without concrete evidence, you're less of a threat. Constable Turley may have done you a considerable favour by removing the shells and manuscript."

"Where are they now?" I persisted.

"Leave it alone," he repeated. "I've told you all I can. We won't talk about this again, and remember I'll deny I told you any of this."

"How about watching me change back into my clothes?" I asked.

"I'll forego that pleasure," he said. "I'm reasonably confident you've not secreted a listening or recording device and I did an electronic sweep of the glider before you saw it."

We were now lined up with a long runway, settling in for

a landing. It was oddly slow and quiet compared with the drama of a powered airplane roaring in to land. I saw braking flaps go up on the wings and we floated down lightly with a barely discernible thump on the single wheel. The wings stayed level for a few seconds and then the left tipped over slowly and dragged as we rolled to a stop.

Harlan unsnapped the canopy and we got out, each taking a wing and rolling the glider toward the hangar. When we'd gotten it into the hangar, I peered into those unnerving blue eyes. I considered my feelings about him. He was a cold mother, certainly responsible for a good helping of death and destruction. But he had a curious integrity, making few excuses for who he was or what he'd done.

"I'll think seriously about your advice," I said. He shook my hand for a moment, said, "Do that," and waited by the glider as I walked back to the barracks and changed.

When I mounted my bike and roared away, he was still standing there, immoveable. Tomorrow, he would be dead.

Chapter Fourteen

Mar and I had a delicious dinner, with small but very artfully designed courses. With the indulgence of our waiter, we sat in a small loft upstairs, occupying the only table there. That way we could enjoy ourselves without her worrying about who would notice her dining with a stranger. I updated her on what I'd learned during my first glider flight.

We decided to spend the night apart, as she had to get up early for her next shift. I had planned a nice little sleeping-in morning for myself, but it didn't happen.

The phone did its tinny version of the Talking Heads again, but this time Mar sounded uncharacteristically tense.

"You'd better get over here right away. William Harlan's been shot dead in his house and you're probably one of the last people to speak to him." This woke me up fast; I put the coffee on while I showered and dressed in near-record time. I was at the scene in less than an hour.

Harlan's body, zipped into a bag, was being wheeled away to a van on a gurney when I arrived.

I waved to Mar as I got off my bike, but found another police officer in my face as soon as I took my helmet off. He wore sergeant's stripes and was lean, olive-skinned and definitely not friendly.

"I'm Sergeant Pucci. Who the hell are you, and what are you doing at my crime scene?" he demanded aggressively.

"It's OK, Sergeant." Mar said, approaching us. "This is Aaron Miles. I asked him to come, since he talked with the vic yesterday."

"That so?" Pucci said, relaxing fractionally. "Did you terminate the conversation by shooting him?"

"Not guilty," I said. "I left him at the Picton Flying Club, still alive. I'm sure others at the Club can verify that."

"What were you talking about?" he asked.

"He was giving me some background for a case I'm working on that involves Gavin Owen."

"The deceased Gavin Owen?" Pucci confirmed. "Man, people are just dying like flies around you, aren't they? And how do I know you didn't come back later and shoot him?"

"I was having dinner at a restaurant in Bloomfield last night between 7 and 9 p.m., and then I went home. I'm sure the staff there can confirm my presence," I offered, neglecting to identify my dinner date. Mar looked relieved.

He was distracted by other officers asking him about search patterns around the house.

"Lemieux, take a statement from him," Pucci barked. To me he said, originally. "You, don't touch anything."

He stalked off to supervise what was going on inside the house. The front door hung open, creaking in the breeze. It had two slightly burned holes at chest height.

Mar led me away, took out her notebook, and recorded a just-the-facts version, although we left out some of the details about the past that Harlan had confirmed. We decided that I had interviewed him just to get some background on the history of U.S. intelligence and whether he could confirm Owen's involvement in any operations.

After I'd finished my edited account, Mar looked at me seriously. "Judging by what's happened first to Owen and then Harlan, he had a point. Maybe it is time for you to back off. I don't want to be interviewing witnesses to *your* death next."

I nodded and said I'd certainly think about it. I felt out of my league. I was one guy with no weapons (or weapons training for that matter), up against an apparently well financed, well equipped, and ruthless cabal of shadowy but violent men. What chance did I stand of defending myself against them if they made me the next target? I couldn't even get together a few thousand bucks and a slick lawyer to offer them as a go-away bribe to the opposition.

The search of the grounds was winding down. Investigators had cast a few tire tracks and photographed debris in the yard. They didn't do much inside, since it appeared likely the perp had never entered; the front door had still been locked when a keen-eyed neighbour had noticed the holes in it and called the police in.

"The old guy sure had a fancy electronic security system," said one of the evidence techs on his way out. "Too bad it didn't stop bullets."

That reminded me of Harlan's super-careful nature. I'd bet he had more ways of observing who was at the front door than just his little spyhole.

I surveyed the front of the house and noticed one anomaly: a fancy light hanging from a black metal stem a few feet above and to the right of the door. It had an oddly faceted globe over its bulb, looking like a transparent pineapple. Everything else about the front of the house was rigorously symmetrical, down to the bushes, except this lone lamp.

I motioned the evidence tech over and said, "Did you look inside that light?"

He gave me a bored expression, and seemed about to flip me off when Mar stepped in. "Do it," she said.

He fetched a ladder from the side of his van, reached up, and carefully unscrewed the globe. Looking inside, he whistled, and held up a tiny black box. "Video surveillance camera," he said, "with a motion sensor and wireless link. Very state of the art. This must be recorded on a DVR somewhere in the house."

It took me a moment to decode the jargon: DVR must be a digital video recorder.

A search of a closet turned up a previously unnoticed black box connected to a wireless receiving unit. The tech popped an SD flash card out of the unit, and inserted it into a laptop sitting on the dining room table. We all watched in silence as a van labeled "County Gas" pulled up and a sunglasses-wearing man in coveralls, a tool belt, and a hard hat got out and approached the door. Given Sergeant Pucci's attitude towards me, I was pleased to note that the suspect was taller and heavier than I. The tech froze the frame and did something to the laptop to zoom in on the license plate, which was easily legible.

Then he started the video playing again and we watched in suspense as the "worker" used the knocker, waited, said something, and then pulled out a large revolver and shot twice right through the door. He took a rag from his pocket, wiped the knocker where he had touched it, and drove off. After running a minute more, the recording shut down.

"Right," Pucci said, and turned to me. "You know, Miles, this is usually a quiet place for homicides. We have a couple a year, and they're pretty easy to solve; domestic disputes, disagreements over drugs, low-level stuff. We don't go in for contract killings or biker wars around here.

"And now we've got three suspicious deaths in under two weeks. Perez and Harlan are definitely murder vics; Owen is beginning to look like one too. I'm calling in help from the Criminal Investigation Branch. I want you around for any questions they might have." I nodded.

"But maybe we can save time for them and us. You're a PI, so by definition you know more than you're telling. How do these killings relate to whatever you're into up here?"

"You know I can't breach client confidentiality unless the client agrees or I'm forced to by a court order." I replied. "I'll help in any way I can with these investigations, except for what my client has paid me to look into."

"We'll see," Pucci said, and made a shooing gesture. "Now buzz off, but leave us a way to reach you any time. And don't get shot without my permission." Amazing. Even Pucci had a sense of humour, if a well-concealed one.

I made a big show of writing out my cell number and giving it to Mar, who thanked me gravely.

I rode out of Harlan's driveway with a sense of foreboding. I decided that I'd best stay somewhere not so easily located or breached as Owen's house.

Chapter Fifteen

So it was back to the no-tell motel for another restless night. The next morning, I heard on local radio that the police had arrested an unnamed suspect in the murder of Harlan. Apparently he had been pulled over just as he was about to cross the bridge on Hwy. 49 near Deseronto. There were no other details offered.

My guess is that he wouldn't be talking, at least not until he knew what kind of case the OPP could build against him. I had a leisurely, over-caloried breakfast. I was wondering if it was time to return to Toronto when my cell phone rang.

I checked the caller ID, which simply read "Private Number." I answered and heard, to my surprise, Sarah's voice. She sounded tense and frightened.

"Aaron, what have you gotten me into?" she asked.

"What do you mean?" I replied. "Nothing, as far as I know. Are you back in Toronto?"

"No, I'm in New York. These men have..."

Suddenly a deeper voice cut in.

"We've got your bitch. You've got 24 hours to bring us what we're looking for from Owen's place, or she's dead." How had they found her? Someone must have been on me in Toronto, tracking my calls, following me to make the connection.

"I thought you already had what you wanted – the shells, his manuscript. That's all I found."

"Holding out on us would be dumb," the voice continued. I heard a little scream in the background, then soft sobbing. "She'll get a lot worse than that if you don't come through."

"Listen," I said desperately, "Don't hurt Sarah. She's got

nothing to do with this case. But I honestly don't have any more evidence to trade for her."

"The movie, asshole," he said. "That's what we want."

"You mean a movie on video? On film? What movie?"

"You'll know it when you see it," he said flatly.

Cutting off any further questions, he started to give me directions to a meeting place in upstate New York.

"Hold on," I interjected, thinking furiously. "Even if I can find this movie, I'm not doing the trade at some secluded farmhouse. It has to be somewhere public, or you guys will just waste us both. Isn't that your style, tying up loose ends? "

To my surprise, he laughed. "You got a point." We agreed on a fast-food restaurant at a thruway service center – the first one south of Pulaski on Interstate 81.

He said, "Meet us there at 1100 hours there, or goodbye, girlfriend. And don't call any of your pals in law enforcement, either. If we even smell a cop, she dies." He hung up.

This trumped Pucci's command for me to stay in the County until their inquiries were completed.

I ran to my bike and fished my map collection out of a saddlebag. I had a decent map that showed both upstate New York and southern Ontario. There was Pulaski. If I went east on Hwy. 401 past Kingston, I could take the Thousand Islands Parkway into New York.

I figured that my bike was not the best way to pick Sarah up. Assuming I could find this movie and trade it for her, she'd be wrung out, not up to a long trip on a motorcycle. Plus, two of us on it were a lot more vulnerable than one – we'd be slower, less maneuverable, a bigger target. Even if they let us get away initially, it's not that hard to run a motorcycle off the road and make it look like an accident. I made a couple of quick calls.

Renting a car and then taking it into the States was complicated, with two sets of insurance to pay for. Some rental companies wouldn't allow it. But the last one I contacted suggested that renting a car once I was over the border would be a lot simpler. I agreed, and booked a Mustang GT350H in Waterdown. This sizable upstate city I knew only from occasional TV watching, when outlandish home-made political and car dealer commercials would interrupt a show.

The Mustang cost about four times the rate of a regular sedan. But it had 330 horsepower and beefed-up suspension. It was the fastest thing on four wheels I could rent at short notice. The investment would be modest if it saved our lives.

Then I checked out in record time and raced over to Owen's house.

I had already done a pretty thorough search of the ground and second floors by now. The only movies I noticed were in his collection of videocassettes, which I flipped through rapidly. They were all feature films or documentaries, and each of the tapes inside the boxes claimed to be the title advertised. I didn't have the time to play each one to verify it wasn't some secret tape labeled to look like a commercial product. I was pinning my hope on the kidnapper's telling the truth when he said I'd know it when I saw it.

Checking the time, I began to sweat. I'd already used up an hour of Sarah's allotment, and I figured I was looking at least three road hours to get to the meet.

OK, time to use my imagination. If this movie were so valuable to my enemies, Owen would hardly leave it anywhere obvious. I did a rapid circuit of first the ground and then second floor, looking for loose or hollow floorboards, checking behind pictures, pulling out books I hadn't looked at yet to make sure none of them were hollowed out.

Nothing.

I hadn't searched the basement carefully yet. However, I had spent some time there, and knew everything was pretty functional: a workbench, a table saw, a drill press, some tools, an oil furnace, a water heater, and some junk. The walls were stone, which made it hard to hide anything in them, and the floor was gravel over dirt. I found a shovel and tossed gravel around for a few minutes, but no hiding places appeared.

I stopped as a thought struck me. Was there an attic? I hadn't seen a door to one, but most older houses had at least a half-assed attic. Upstairs, in the bedroom closet, I found a hatch in the ceiling that I had missed earlier. I went back downstairs and got a flashlight.

Grabbing a chair and stacking a couple of thick books on top of it, I found I could get the hatch open. Then I noticed a step ladder learning against the wall. After I'd shaken off loose insulation which descended on me, I grabbed the hatch edges and levered myself up into the attic.

It was dimly lit by sun slanting through ventilation lattices at one end. There were boxes, old framed pictures and small furniture pieces stored up here – end tables; planters. I opened and upended the half dozen cardboard boxes: nothing but books and papers, as far as I could see. Fascinating as it might have been to read Owen's old tax returns, I didn't have time.

My subconscious started to tug at me. It was nice to know that the inner holistic detective hadn't been killed off by all this drama. Find the anomaly, I thought. What doesn't belong up here?

Behind a large picture wrapped in brown paper, I spotted something that seemed out of place. It was a dusty guitar case. No-one had ever mentioned Owen having a musical gift. Perhaps one day he'd tried to play "The Ould Orange Flute."

I pried up the greening brass catches on the case and extracted a cheap old Japanese six-string. Some of the strings were loose and the neck was bowing. I looked in the case's little cubby for storing picks and capos, but it was empty. Then I picked up the guitar. Its balance felt off, the body a little heavier than it should be.

Trying to feel around in the sound hole didn't work at first. My hand was too big for the space left by the strings. So I popped out the bridge pins with the flat side of my pen-knife's blade.

Now I could get my hand in. Sure enough, I felt a flat package taped next to the sound hole. I cut the tape carefully with the penknife and wrestled it out.

Inside a faded yellow cardboard box was a thin reel of film with tiny images. I guessed it was 8mm, the same format as the famous Abraham Zapruder movie of JFK's assassination. Super 8, if memory served me, hadn't been introduced by Kodak until 1965, two years after Kennedy died. This had to be what they wanted. But surely it wasn't another movie of the assassination? There were enough reporters and observers around Dealey Plaza that Zapruder, for example, had been seen by several witnesses. Anyone else with a movie camera would have been noted.

I thought quickly. I had more than enough time to get to Watertown, park my bike, pick up the rental car, and make it to the meet. Once I handed the film over, I'd have no edge over the bad guys, and extricating Sarah and myself safely would be difficult.

There was no film projector in this house, or I would have seen it by now. Also no Yellow Pages, which rather went with the no-phone theme of the house.

I used my laptop to check listings for Belleville and got lucky. There was a camera and audio-visual place that offered transfers of 8 and 16mm film to DVD, and it was open. I left Mar a message saying I'd be on a trip to New York State for a few days. I thought it better not to mention Pucci's directive at all; maybe she hadn't heard him give it.

Then I sat down at my laptop and whipped off a quick letter to my lawyer in Toronto, saying that I was mailing a DVD to him for insurance, and in the event of my death or disappearance, it should be turned over to Constable Lemieux of the Prince Edward OPP. With some fumbling, I managed to get the old dot matrix printer to spit out a hard copy.

Locking up the house, I headed to Belleville and reached the store in half an hour.

I had 21 hours left. Fortunately, 8mm films are short – this one ran only five minutes or so. The store owner, a friendly Pakistani fellow, set up his equipment, and ran off a couple of DVD copies for me. When he was done, I asked 'if we could view the film. He looked at me oddly, having assumed this was some much-loved bit of my family history, but agreed. The film was silent, but nonetheless very educational.

It had two sequences. In the first, the man I had come to recognize as Lucien Sarti was filmed calibrating his rifle sights, and trying various rounds of ammunition on watermelons balanced on a set of sawhorses at various distances. The watermelons disintegrated, reminding me of the grim frames of the Zapruder film.

A longer sequence that followed showed Sarti and a couple of other men I didn't know. They were walking around Dealey Plaza, looking through binoculars, pointing to various landmarks and gesturing with their hands. One was making notes on a pad. I realized with a chill that they were working out the best locations to place three shooters and triangulate the President's limousine as it rolled along the widely publicized route. Sarti and his accomplices were cocky, expansive. They smiled broadly for the camera, even waved to a police officer in shades who was patrolling the sidewalks. Not knowing how history was going to change soon, anyone watching these men would have thought they were tourists, or maybe cut-rate urban planners.

As the film approached its end, the camera pulled back jerkily, and a couple more men were included in the frame. They were talking, not looking at the camera, and it was hard to make out their features in the grainy frames. Then the last frame ran out and the film wound around on the projector, flapping, until the store owner switched it off.

I looked at him. He appeared unperturbed; probably he didn't know where Dealey Plaza was.

I paid him and then bought a padded envelope and mailed one DVD and the letter to my lawyer in Toronto.

There's not much to tell about the trip to Waterdown. I had to wait about fifteen minutes to cross into the USA, so I guess cross-border shopping is still a reality. When Immigration asked me the purpose of my visit, I said "Pleasure and shopping." I neglected to mention that I was trading, for one very frightened librarian, a film that might prove the assassination of their 43rd president was a conspiracy.

I was pleased to see that it was only about fifty miles from Waterdown to Pulaski. Miles, my very own name – when was the last time I had seen that on a road sign? America, with its usual charming assurance that it knows best, is now the only developed nation *not* on the Metric system.

I made it to Watertown, and paid the Hertz clerk an extra twenty to let me park my bike at the back of his chain-link-fenced lot. The Mustang was black with gold stripes and made the right noises.

I checked into a cheap motel where I could keep an eye on the car out my front window. All I needed was for some local hood to steal my wheels.

The first thing on my list was a weapon of some kind. So I went into the first sports store I could find. They were friendly, but couldn't sell me a Taser (illegal for citizens in NY), and handgun purchases required a licence with up to six months waiting – even if I were a U.S. citizen. Then I looked around the store and spotted a skin diving equipment section. It reminded me of those great underwater fight sequences in James Bond movies.

"How about a spear gun?" I asked. "Sure, we can sell you one of those right away," the clerk said. "October's not the best time for spear fishing around here, though."

I said, "Don't ask, and I won't tell," and forked over the better part of $100 for what he described as a good utility/beginners' carbine spear gun. It had ABS stock and grips, and was about a meter long, which meant I could grab it out of the backseat faster than the full sized one with its long stocks. Pulling the giant elastic band back to cock it was hard, but I could do it. I knew there was a reason I'd taken to working out on rowing machines the last few years.

I stopped by a convenience store and picked up a couple of bottles of water and a few items I thought might be useful in a pinch: a disposable cigarette lighter, a can of lighter fluid, a pack of J-cloths.

I had a Denny's dinner, went back to the motel, and tried to grab some rest. I was too wound up and worried to sleep well, though. I ended up watching the usual disasters on CNN for a while, then a late night televangelist with a wolfish expression and a backup choir in gauzy gold robes. Then I saw most of the 1953 movie *Houdini*, with Tony Curtis. Tony was pretty good, actually, and by the way he always denied ever saying "Yonda lies da castle of my fadduh" in another movie. I'll take his word for it.

I woke up at 7:00, stiff and cold in the armchair. Sunlight was edging over the trees. A long semi-hot shower loosened up my muscles, and I went for an energy breakfast: eggs over easy, bacon, toast, and hash browns.

I packed my meagre belongings, checked out, and looked at my watch. I only had a half hour to get to know my rental, so I bought a road map at the first service station I spotted.

I found a secondary road that looked promising, running

roughly parallel to the Interstate. After I got past the last mall, I opened the Mustang up. It had power, no doubt about it. But the older Mustangs I'd driven cornered about as well as a wheelbarrow holding a V-8 engine. This one was a lot better. The body motions were well damped, and it didn't lean much on corners. With a little practice, I found I could use the throttle and brakes to load and unload the back end in corners, producing a nice little power slide that got the rear wheels around and lined up for the next corner. I had to admit that, for a rental Ford, this was a pretty solid car.

I cut back onto the Interstate at the next exchange and got to the service center a few minutes early. I cruised the lot first, not seeing anything out of the ordinary; none of the pick-ups, SUVs, station wagons and sedans parked there had rocket launchers or .50 cal machine guns mounted on them.

I parked the car nose out, grabbed the film from under the floor mat, tucked it into my jacket, and walked in. I saw no Sarah. Ordering a coffee, I took a booth at the back and sat facing the entrance.

Chapter Sixteen

At about 10:06, Sarah appeared. Her captors had probably spent a few minutes inspecting the other vehicles, just as I had, with an eye out for anything that looked like surveillance. There was a large blond guy on her left holding her arm, and a medium-sized dark-haired one on her right with his hand in his jacket pocket. The message was obvious.

I stood up and Sarah saw me. She looked pale and tired, but managed a tentative smile. The three walked up to my booth and Sarah and the shorter thug sat across from me. The big blond guy told me to take off my jacket, and then was last in, barely able to fit onto what was left of the bench. I took the jacket off and folded it on the table. Blondie leaned over and patted under my arms and then reached around to the small of my back. I could smell his after-shave; it made Old Spice seem a luxury brand. He gave me a medium-hard punch in the gut, too, a nasty short jab that took my breath away for a minute. I guess that's what they consider softening up the enemy. Sarah said my name.

I reached out for her hand, but the smaller guy slapped it away contemptuously.

"No touching the merchandise, asshole, until we see what you've got."

"She's hardly merchandise," I replied. "She's worth a lot more than both of you, or any movie."

I handed over the faded Eastman Kodak box. The dark-haired guy grunted, turned the reel over in his hands, then pulled out a jeweller's loupe and held a few frames of the film up to the light filtering through the none-too-clean window. Apparently, it fit what he'd been told to look for.

He nodded. "That's it, all right. Take your bitch and go."

I stood up, and shrugged on my jacket. Blondie stood up to let Sarah pass, and grabbed her ass once as she pushed by him. Then I slowly reached into my inner pocket and extracted the second DVD copy I'd had made.

"In appreciation for your beautiful manners," I started, while they stared at me, nonplussed, "I've got another little present for you."

"The hell's this?" the blonde one asked, frowning.

"It's a DVD case," I said. "Inside you'll find a disk – that'll surprise you – with a copy of the movie I just gave you. There's also a copy of the letter I sent to my lawyer with another disk. Unfortunately, I left his name and address off this copy. With the help of a dictionary and an hour or two, though, you should be able to figure out the rest of the letter."

I draped my arm over Sarah's shoulders, and we walked out the door. She said she was tired, but OK; they'd pawed her a few times, and pinched her arm hard during the phone call to me, but otherwise she'd been left alone.

I apologized as best I could to her, saying this wasn't the thanks I'd planned for her. Then I gave her a very compressed version of the story and explained what was on the film that I'd traded for her. She looked disbelieving, then I saw the light of curiosity come back into her tired eyes. If there's one thing a talented researcher can't resist, it's a good mystery.

I glanced behind me to see that they had followed us to the door, no doubt to check what I was driving. They launched into a brief argument, waving arms and pointing at each other, and then dark-hair made a "shut up" gesture and pulled out a smartphone. As we got into the Mustang, they finally came through the door and walked quickly to a dark, medium-sized SUV; it looked like a Mercedes. Where was the buy-American spirit, I wondered. If even heavies working for ultra-right-wing conspiracies in the U.S. weren't driving Detroit iron, the country was going down the toilet, just like Harlan had said.

I checked my rear-view mirror, and saw Blondie take the wheel. His partner was obviously getting updated orders. As we sped onto the service road leading back onto the thruway, I saw a second SUV pull up behind the other one. As I'd anticipated, they had friends.

It wasn't far to the next interchange, and I booted the Mustang, spinning the tires until the first automatic upshift and breaking the speed limit by about thirty of those old-fashioned miles per hour. I took the cloverleaf as fast as I could. I figured the opposition would expect me to circle around and come back on the Interstate heading for Canada. No way. On a multi-lane highway, they just had to wait for slow traffic to get in my way, and then they could box me in with their two vehicles and force us off the road. Or just shoot us. From what I'd seen in the County, their outfit had no qualms about using guns.

No, as I told Sarah, I liked our odds a lot better on a curvy two-laner, where the lumbering SUVs would be hard pressed to keep up with us on the corners.

I screeched onto a rural highway, cutting ahead of an elderly man in a Buick. I waved in apology and then goosed the accelerator again. I could see the twin SUVs coming up behind the Buick, but they had a double line beside them and oncoming traffic. I wanted to make the most of our chance to win some space. The SUVs got around the Buick and came up close behind, though, when I was slowed by a long truck in front of me and a school bus in the oncoming lane. The Mercedes behind us gave us a little "Guess who's here?" thump on the bumper.

I checked the traffic and barely made it around the big semi rig, sliding back into the right lane seconds before a horn-blasting dump truck almost flattened us. I glanced over at Sarah; her eyes were closed, and I think she was actually praying.

There was a temporary gap in the traffic. Bad news. Also, I saw a sharp, almost hairpin turn ahead that paralleled an oxbow in the river. One of the SUVs charged ahead on me on the left. I could have out-accelerated it, but I remembered something from an evasive driver course a client had paid me to attend a while ago: the Pursuit Intervention Technique or PIT Maneuver.

The SUV cut in ahead of me and started to slow down. The other one was pulling up to sit on my bumper, so the two of them could block and force me off the road. But I gave the leader a taste of my front bumper, pushing him against the force of his brakes. We were just about in the corner now. I swung my car to the inside of the corner and tapped the left rear of the SUV. A lot of drivers of those ungainly vehicles think that because they do have more traction in a straight line, they do on turns too.. But they're overweight and top heavy, a combination that makes for cornering worse than the average car's. Sure enough, the driver ahead lost control. His Mercedes spun backwards and into the river before he could correct the skid.

I could see in my rear view that the second driver was still behind me. But I liked the odds better now.

Then I cut to the inside on a curve to the right and saw something ahead that gave me an idea. A farmer pulling a big load of late hay with his giant tractor turned slowly into our lane about a half a mile ahead.

I reached behind me and dumped the bag from the convenience store in her lap.

"Sarah," I said, as I raced towards the hay rig. "Take out a J-cloth, and soak it in lighter fluid. Then take the spear gun – careful with the safety, don't let it off – and tie the rag around the spear head."

She looked at me quizzically but did what I asked. I checked the rear view mirror. The SUV was gaining on us. I could smell the sweet hay, and really regretted what I was about to do; farmers, I knew, worked harder for less money than most people.

I took the spear gun by its handle and told Sarah to get ready with the cigarette lighter. I powered down the passenger-side window. Having guessed what I was up to, she quickly put the bag with the remaining lighter fluid back behind us. Sensible person.

Then I accelerated up beside the hay wagon and hit the brakes. "Light it," I yelled.

The rag puffed up a burst of orange flame. I clicked the safety off with my thumb and fired the spear into the hay.

Then I hammered the throttle again and pulled ahead of the hay rig, narrowly missing a pickup truck coming the other way. This has to be the busiest two-laner in New York State, I thought.

I watched in my rear view mirror. The bale I'd skewered caught and began to burn, spilling thick grey smoke behind it. I could see the SUV come up behind the trailer and then disappear in the haze. The farmer apparently hadn't noticed anything amiss yet; he had headphones clamped on his ears, probably to cut the roar of his diesel engine, and was bobbing his John Deere cap back and forth to an unheard beat.

My mind is a curious thing. What popped into it at that moment when we were being chased by murderers and I'd just vandalized a hay wagon? An old joke: how did the farmer's wife tell him she was leaving him for another man? She sent him a John Deere letter. However, my right foot was staying on task, and we were doing well over 100 mph by now, the SUV far behind and invisible in the smoke.

Watching my rear view, I took the second crossroad, raced down it, around a couple of curves, and then pulled in beside an abandoned farmhouse flanked by a line of poplar trees. We couldn't be seen from the main road; they'd have to come right down here.

I reloaded our only weapon with another spear and we waited. Sarah entertained herself by locating our position on the GPS unit and cross referencing the map until she knew where we were.

"Figure out a route on back roads to Ogdensburg," I said. "We'll take the bridge across to Prescott."

"Why not the Thousand Islands Bridge?" she asked. "Isn't that closer?"

"Yeah, it's closer," I confirmed. "Which means that, if they stake out a border crossing to watch for us, that's the natural choice. I'd rather cross where they're less likely to be watching."

She nodded. We'd been waiting for ten minutes now, and no sign of any Mercedes SUV. I figured they had continued on the two-laner, convinced we were well ahead of them.

I cautiously nosed back onto the rural highway, but still saw no thug-carrying Benzes. We drove back over the Interstate and then headed east towards Ogdensburg.

As I'd half expected, my cell phone rang. I knew they had forced the number out of Sarah. The display, of course, said Private Caller.

"Let me guess," I said. "Medium-sized thug, short brown hair?"

"Negative, Mr. Miles," an unfamiliar male voice with the distinctive vowels of New England said. "I'm their controller."

"Yeah, they need some control," I rejoined. "What do you want? Make it quick... I'm not staying on long enough for you to track me."

"What do you plan to do with that other DVD copy you claim to have of the film."

"No 'claim' about it," I said. "When you have your goons check out the disk I gave them, you'll know it's a good copy. I made two, and my lawyer has the other one by now."

"It wouldn't take us long to find him or her and eliminate the threat," he said.

"Yeah, and when will you stop eliminating threats?" I asked. "When the entire population of North America has been silenced? You have my word that, as long as Sarah, myself and my lawyer remain unharmed, I will not release the DVD to the public or the police. But go after any of us, and it'll be front-page news all over the world. "JFK Killing Finally Solved!""

He paused for a moment. I concluded, "Think it over," and cut off the connection.

I kept Sarah busy giving me directions – we wove along secondary routes on the shoreline north of the Interstate, until I had the last few turns locked in my memory. "Sleep," I said, kissing her cheek. "I'm going to keep driving until we're safe."

I was a bit worried about crossing back into Canada, as the Mustang was a U.S. rental. We rolled over the Ogdensburg-Prescott bridge, looking down on the broad St. Lawrence.

"Did you know," Sarah said, surprising me as she woke from her nap, "this is the least used of all the Southern Ontario crossings?"

"No, I didn't," I replied. "But thanks for the reference information." She elbowed my side. It was good to see her recovering her usual feistiness.

Fortunately, once the Canadian border guards verified our

Canadian passports, they showed no interest in the car. I guess they didn't know that the H in 350GTH stood for "Hertz."

Chapter Seventeen

Then came the false peace. I got Sarah safely back to Toronto. We agreed there was no point in reporting her kidnapping to the authorities, because answering their questions would lead to disclosure of at least some of the information we'd agreed to sit on.

She'd been silent for a while. We got out of the car and walked to the door of her house. She turned and looked me in the eyes, biting her lip. I knew something was wrong. Deliberately, she raised her hands and pulled me to her by the lapels of my jacket. She offered a lingering kiss, then pushed me away, her hands flat on my chest.

"What is it?" I asked.

"You know I love you…" she began, as my heart sank. "But I need some time. These last few days have been too much for me."

"I know," I empathized. "I'm so sorry I got you mixed up in this, however inadvertently. I never would have taken the case if I'd seen this coming."

"I know," she replied. "It's what we can't see coming that gets us, isn't it?"

I nodded, kept quiet. She was considering some kind of decision… until I knew what it was, no point in trying to influence it.

Above us, a sudden honking medley – more Canada geese heading south.

"I know what you're wondering," she blurted out, "Is there someone else in my life? The answer's no; at least, no one I care about like you. The point is … I want to make sure I have a life. Being taken hostage, and then rescued by a knight on a – well, not white charger, it was more a black Mustang – is too much like a movie. I'd rather watch the DVD.

"You're a good man, Aaron. Sensitive, smart, but not a wimp. I love your poetry, and I appreciate the way you let me be myself. You don't try to take me over. But I need some time to think about us. You can't guarantee that the next case you take won't come back on us again. Give me a few months. In the meantime, if you decide to make your living in a less risky way, call me. Otherwise, I'll call when I can't stay away any longer.

"That's the deal. Or, you can just walk away. We're both adults; we'll survive somehow."

I looked at her catlike eyes. A tear trembled at the edge of each. "I'll take Option A. You're too good to give up on. Call me when you're ready." We hugged. I tried to store that sense memory of her firm body and honey-scented hair as she turned away, and gently closed the door behind her.

I drove away, both sad – I'd miss Sarah fiercely– and somehow relieved. If we were not seen together for a while, any backlash from the cabal that had snatched her would probably fall on me, not her. I could live with that.

I took care of some business. First, I drove the Mustang back over the border to the rental agency, and rode my bike home. My back hurt from the ride, but I have endured worse penances. Nobody bothered me.

I retrieved the DVD from my lawyer, double-locked my door, and spent a couple of obsessive hours watching it, again and again. OK, so *mon vieux ami* Lucien and his buddies once again walked around Dealey Plaza and he slaughtered a few watermelons. That, in itself, proved nothing.

Then, my subconscious rang one of those chimes that sounds like a church bell hidden in the chords of Debussy's piano piece about the drowned cathedral. What was so important about the unknown guy with the high brow and jut-jaw? I realized it was because I'd seen him before. But where?

So I pawed through the files I'd assembled on the JFK killing, in the hopes of finally confirming whether Gavin was putting me on or leading me to something approaching the truth.

One of the issues around JFK's death that fed the conspiracy theorist machine was how sloppy the Secret Service agents had been, how slow to react when the first shot was fired on that fateful November day. Their highest duty is to protect the POTUS (President of the United States); they're programmed to take the bullet themselves. Yet, in the seven seconds or so over which the shots were fired, only one Secret Service agent notably reacted ... the one who clung onto the rear of Kennedy's Lincoln as the traumatized Jackie reached back to him. Where were the others who normally take positions on the running boards, so that snipers' views are obstructed? Why was one agent in a following car photographed with a strange smile on his face just before the shooting?

I flipped through the prints I'd made, photos of the President's entourage before the first shot. Damn... there he was! One of the agents in a following car, perhaps then-Vice President Johnson's, had his face partly obscured. But I recognized the brow and jaw. It was the guy from Sarti's home movie.

He had to be in on the conspiracy to have been walking around the Plaza with them. No doubt his role was to give the shooters intel on the likely speed and sequencing of the convoy so that they could plan their firing positions for the best chance of success.

So finally I had it... the smoking gun. A conspiracy had reached into the elite bodyguard that was supposed to shield Presidents. The untouchable Secret Service had been bought out. Keep your friends close, but your enemies closer, the old saying goes. Kennedy hadn't known how close he was keeping at least one enemy.

The siren call of fame and fortune echoed in my ears. With the DVD of the film, the photographs, and Gavin's memoir, I could name my price for a book that would sell in *50 Shades of Grey* numbers. I'd be rich. Public interest in JFK had, if anything, intensified with the election of the new President, a man who brought hope, youth, and new style to the White House. The institution's reputation had suffered badly under the arrogant frat-boy Republicans who had run it for the previous eight years. Like

Kennedy, the new POTUS had an attractive, fashionable wife, kids young enough to be cute, and was riding a populist wave from grassroots citizens who had done the unthinkable: elected someone different from the white guys who had a lock on the Presidency since George Washington's wooden teeth first bit into it.

Or did they? Are you aware that the website mountvernon.org says "It's quite possible that some of his dentures, particularly after they had been stained, took on a wooden complexion, but wood was never used in the construction of any of his dental fittings. Throughout his life Washington employed numerous full and partial dentures that were constructed of materials including bone, hippopotamus ivory, human teeth, brass screws, lead, and gold metal wire." I bet this encouraged George to keep his speeches short.

I felt uncomfortably like I was in one of those old cartoons in which a devil sits on one shoulder, whispering seductively, and then the angel alights on the other with advice less immediately alluring, but which makes more sense in the cold light of eternity.

If I published, there was a good chance I'd perish. Maybe I could disappear to a tax haven somewhere, invest in a little facial reconstruction, and stay off the talk show circuit. But I had little doubt that the avenging forces I'd already stirred up would come after people I cared about when they couldn't find me: Sarah, Mar, my lawyer... God knows who. Unlike me, they didn't appear to suffer from conscience.

So there wasn't really a choice. I'd keep my lips zipped. I snapped the DVD back into its case and decided to rent a safe deposit box in a bank I don't normally use. I'd keep the DVD and my case files there. This would both give me an insurance policy and take the heat off my lawyer.

If he didn't know where the files were and the bad guys knew he didn't know, he'd be safe.

I called Richard and filled him in. There was a shocked silence, and then he said weakly: "Thank God I called you in. You've certainly earned your keep. If this got into the news, we'd never hear the end of it..."

He cleared his throat. "I think, under the circumstances, we'll forego your usual report-poem. The fewer trails leading to this story, the better." I was of the same mind. If there was ever was something I didn't want to write, it was the ballad of Gavin Owen and his misspent youth.

We agreed I'd return to the County and wrap up the clearing out and sale of Richard's house as best I could.

I rented one more car; this time, a nice, bland little compact box. I'd have to draw a map to find it in a crowded parking lot. It did have one compensation: a surprisingly loud and clear CD system. I delighted myself with the intricate finger-picking and fine song-writing skills of Mark Knopfler and his lesser-known compatriot, Martin Simpson, as I put Oshawa, then Port Hope, Coburg, and the Big Apple into my rear view mirror. Once back in the County, I called Mar.

I explained what had happened. She whistled in disbelief.

"Has Pucci missed me?"

"Yeah, he wants to date your ass," she replied. "Seriously, we're in a holding pattern right now. The guy from the van isn't talking – big surprise there – and neither is Turley. They're both going to have their day in court. You might be called as a witness, but Pucci talked to some Toronto cops who know you, and thinks that you're probably clean, as far as Harlan's death goes. So no more questioning, at least until the Crown Attorney starts working on the trials."

We agreed we'd get together soon and I hung up. Taking a little walk back to the woods to stretch my legs, I realized November had snuck up on me again. October has many compensations – clear air, golden light, hints of warmth on sunny days, the kaleidoscopic maple displays. Then, as if a set designer threw a switch, everything turns into Bleak House: grey, wet and gloomy. Out on the Great Lakes, the last big freighters of the season brave sudden gales. I have no doubt every sailor on them thinks about the *Edmund Fitzgerald* and the puzzling speed with which she sank in one of those storms.

The next few days were restfully mundane. Cleaners again, book buyers, house painters, a representative of a local auction firm, and a trash hauler came and went. I was interested in the phenomenon that specialization brings partial blindness: each only saw the part of the house that was their concern. The painter saw books only as nuisances in the way of his ladders; the cleaner saw the grime but not the art on the walls; and so on. All that interested Mr. Trash was the stuff that could be tossed, and what he might be able to resell some of it for.

Once we'd got the house tidied, the real estate lady helped me place a couple of big vases with cut flowers in the open area. The house neither looked nor smelled like the lair of a seedy bachelor any more. In deference to Catholic customers, we took down the sign over the front door, the Orange Order wall banner and the painting of King Billy. I felt a tinge of guilt doing this – sure, Owen was a bigot, but this was his house, the last visible physical vestige of him, anyway. His body was now reposing in the family vault at the Toronto Necropolis.

Then potential buyers came. The third visit was from a middle-aged couple who'd timed the sale of their Vancouver house perfectly, when the market was red hot, and now were sitting on a nest egg that could buy Owen's house, renovate it to their big-city standards, and still leave them comfortably well off. They made an offer, the real estate agent called Richard, and a deal was struck. I was pretty much done here.

But the next day was a gift: sunny, a few degrees above freezing, and almost windless.

I had a sudden inspiration. A restaurant, part of an inn that sits on the edge of Lake on the Mountain. I called, and found they were still open. My next call was to Mar; yes, she could do lunch and would meet me there.

I went behind the house and pulled the tarp off the one possession of Gavin's that Richard didn't want to part with. It was a vintage Chestnut sixteen-foot canoe. Unlike some of his other things, Gavin had kept it in good shape. There was fresh varnish on its amber ribs and newly woven seats. I'd located two paddles and a couple of life jackets in the cellar, so I tossed them into my econo-box and trussed the Chestnut on the roof with a quilt underneath to protect the roof.

I got to the lake a few minutes before Mar, giving me time to unload the canoe and leave it on the shore. I parked in the big lot across the road and watched the toy-like ferry below make waves across the bay between Glenora and the mainland.

We had a good lunch – I've always been partial to good, simple Quebecois cooking, and they served a *tourtière* that fit that description. Then I told Mar I had a little surprise, and led her to the canoe. I'd left the quilt in it to soften the impact of canoe ribs on our knees.

Her eyes widened, and then she helped me slide it into the water. We paddled aimlessly across the lake, watching as the last autumn leaves danced with sunlight in tiny waves. No-one else was on the lake, and there was little sign of life at the homes whose lawns sloped down to the water. We found a big dead tree projecting from a quiet shore, with a screen of bushes behind it. We tied up there and sat on the tree for a few minutes, holding each other and watching the wind shape the water.

"Do you know what Pierre Berton said defined a Canadian?"

"Thinking we won the War of 1812," she ventured.

"It's someone who can make love in a canoe," I said with a straight face.

She stared at me for a moment, and then her lips curved into a smile. Without saying more, she helped me spread the quilt over the bottom and set the life jackets on top as pillows. Balancing awkwardly on the tree trunk, we helped each other off with our pants and underwear. It seemed too late in the year to strip completely.

Giggling, we carefully got in, lay down with our heads toward the bow, and somehow got our legs under the middle thwart. One of the benefits of middle age is that you learn to accept that looking ridiculous does not have to kill an erotic moment. Pierre would have been proud of us, certifying our nationality so late in the year.

We made little waves as we got into it, and then a late loon called across the lake, his whoops echoing between the still woods.

I composed a silent prayer to whatever deity created and guarded the mystery of Mountain on the Lake that all other massive conspiracies would continue without my involvement, and my remaining cases would be quiet little gun-free mysteries. Preferably literary ones. The wind suddenly started up, murmuring something indistinguishable.

Ain't it good to be alive?

About the Author

John Oughton was born in Guelph, Ontario, a block away from the home of John McCrae (author of "In Flanders Fields"). When his father was seconded to the World Health Organization, John spent two years living in Egypt and Iraq. He completed a BA and MA in English at York U., where he studied with Irving Layton, Eli Mandel, Miriam Waddington and Frank Davey. After a half-year stay in Kyoto, Japan, he worked at Coach House Press and as a journalist and corporate communicator. He attended the Jack Kerouac School of Disembodied Poetics at Naropa University, and served as a research assistant to Allen Ginsberg and Anne Waldman. John began teaching English in community colleges, and is now Professor of Learning and Teaching at Centennial College.

He has published five books of poetry, most recently Time Slip (Guernica Editions, 20190), several chapbooks, and over 400 articles, interviews, reviews and blogs. John is a long-time member of the Long Dash writing workshop. He is also a photographer with three solo shows and several book and magazine covers to his credit. For fun, he plays guitar and drums. Until recently, he did ride an old Yamaha motorcycle.

photograph by Sue MacLeod

NeoPoiesis: *a new way of making*

1) in ancient Greece, poiesis referred to the
process of making: creation - production -
organization - formation - causation

2) a process that can be physical and
spiritual, biological and intellectual,
artistic and technological, material and
teleological, efficient and formal

3) a means of modifying the environment
and a method of organizing the self,
the making of art and music and poetry,
the fashioning of memory and history and
philosophy, the construction of perception
and expression and reality

4) an independent publisher with a steadfast
goal to print and promote outstanding
poets, writers and artists that reflect
the creative drive and spirit of the new
electronic landscape

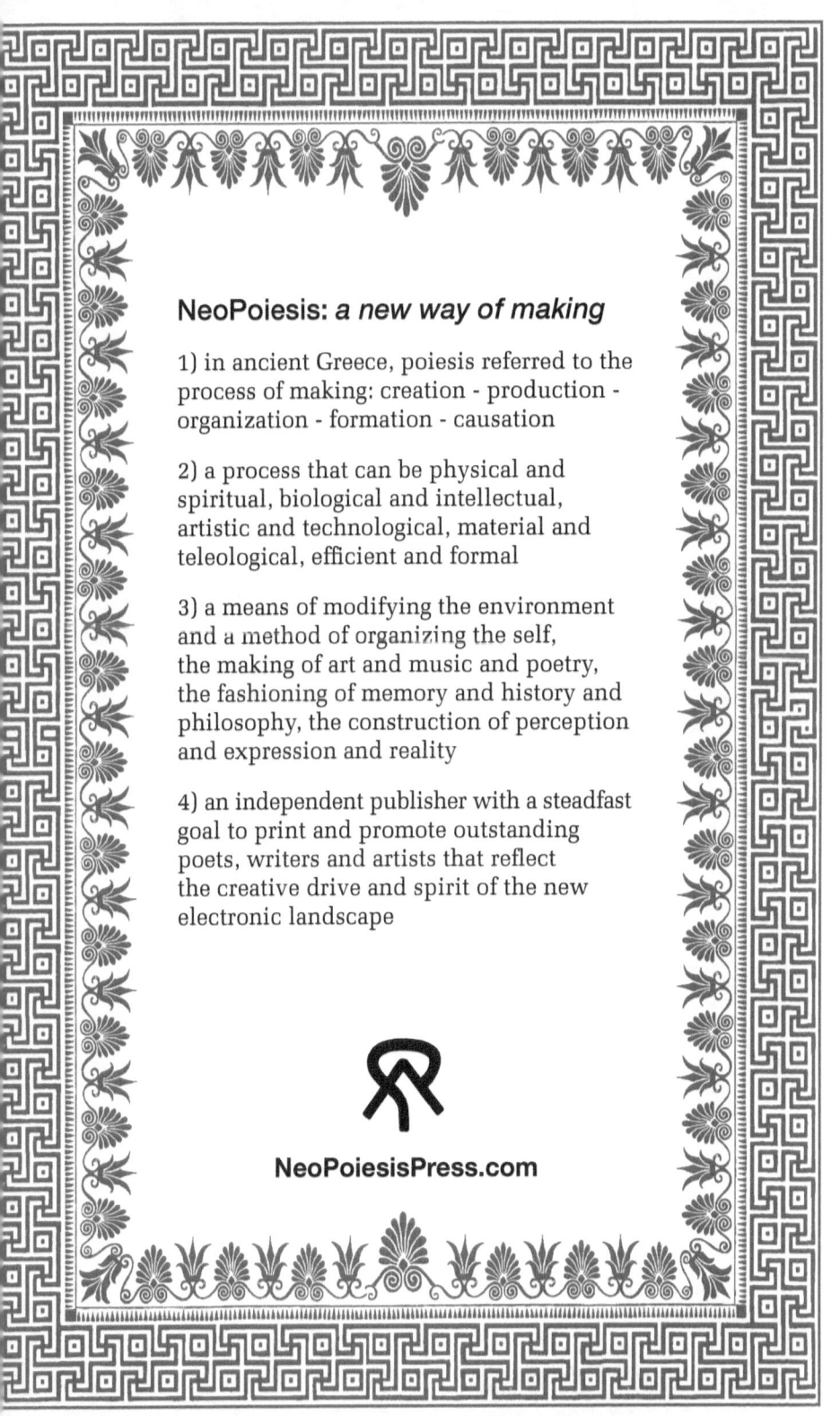

NeoPoiesisPress.com